The Long Short

By Michael Lachance

The Long Short by Michael Lachance

Skipper Pete Books, PO Box 16, Glenwood, IA 51534

Print ISBN: 978-1370672103

Contents

Chapter 1: Paris, France

Present day:

Bill was on time in his twenties, if he had an appointment at one o'clock, he was there at ten minutes till one o'clock; it was a military thing, but when he got out of the military he got out of the habit of getting to places early. In his thirties, he was more halfhearted and it showed in his work and life.

"I know you like to take your time to get dressed, but even I have a point where it's too much." Bill looked at the door to his grandmother's bedroom.

In her room, French jazz played and she turned the volume up.

His grandmother's accent was thick and she rolled her "r's" with perfection. Her strong cheeks and soft lips, she believed, drew from a distant relation to Sophia Loren. She took that into consideration every time she dressed. She did her makeup without any concern for time, a couple of hours to try on dresses that were fashionable and whatever time it took to go through her perfumes for the most appropriate scent. She was a perfectionist and time did not interfere with beauty.

He pulled at his dress shirt and looked down at his gut which looked back up at him. "So, I'm a little overweight." He rubbed his belly. "I'm not chunky, grandma." He shouted at the door and pushed his bangs from his face. "I have muscles."

The door opened and she stood there. "Oui, mais qu'est-ce que vous faites avec les muscles?" She looked him over.

"J'ai compris, okay." He said.

"No, it's not okay. You speak French all the way or you speak English all the way." She shook her head. "You speak Franglais, that is not okay." She looked at his hair. "Your hair is French, thick and brown, like Sophia Loren. Try to take care of yourself; this is not just a French thing."

"Okay, don't start that." He looked at the ceiling.

"Americans eat like it is their last meal." She waved her hands in slow jabs. "One pound of fried chicken, potatoes that are fried."

"There's a frit stand just up the street, grandma." He smiled heartily.

"Frits!" She raised her brow. "This is a Belgian thing, not a French thing." She scoffed, went to the chaise, and sat down.

"Whatever," he said jokingly and sat next to her.

"Whatever, another American word that is better left to your mind and not your mouth." She said. "And why so many jobs for you?" She looked him over. "You look and behave like you don't care."

"No stress at work means I have hair on my head." He got up and moved his carryon to the door.

"You are like the American's say, jack of all trades and master of none." She got her scarf around her neck; tan and peach were good colors for her fair skin. "And you do ten days in that." She looked at his carryon and got up. "This is for paupers to travel like that; my grandson is no pauper."

He mumbled, "flying basic coach." Then, he looked his carryon over. "We're going to be late."

"Worry about your life, not the time." She came down the steps to the front door. "In France, this is what we mean when we say …"

"C'est la vie." He said.

"One complete French sentence." A semi-surprised look came over her face.

"This is my last night in Paris, grandma." His heart warmed as it sped up.

"Alors, parle tu Francais." She stood at the door, turned and looked at him. "Je t'aime Bill, mais je ne comprends pas comment tu aller d'une chose à l'autre. Je n'ai jamais eu dix emplois en dix ans."

"You say my French isn't very good." He frowned. "I love you too." He went to her and they hugged. "And I've had eight jobs in ten years, not ten jobs, because I work short contracts." He opened the door, walked out and held the door. "I like to know and do different things."

"Find one thing and focus." She said. "You may have a choice to do it and better your life."

"Bien sur," he gave her a kiss and they went to dinner.

The next morning, he woke and looked himself over in a closet mirror, "no one's pretty at this hour."

Grandma came out dressed in flats, sleek jeans and a rose-colored blouse.

"That's chic for the morning, France." He got his phone out. "Let's do a selfie."

"Selfie, to hear that word gives me a headache." She did her best smile and tilted her head just so her rosy cheeks shined. "Okay," she said and shook her finger at the phone.

The phone made a click and then another. "Two … just in case." He looked the pictures over and smiled, "nice."

"Agréable," she looked at the image.

"Alright, I love …" He said.

"S'il te plait, William." She puckered her lips.

"Je t'aime grand-mére." They kissed, hugged and then he was out the door, "au-revoir."

"Au-revoir, mon cher petit fils," she wiped her eyes and watched him walk down the Parisian street with his carryon in tow.

Paris, Charles De Gaulle was a melee of nationalities that rushed from this place to that place. Announcements began with a soft bell that sounded three times followed by a lovely French woman's voice, "Faites attention," and then she went on to tell the passengers about gate changes.

Bill made his way through security and then to his gate, "A 37." The walk went on and on and on. Until he found another sign, "A 37" with an arrow. "Really," he muttered and then forced himself to look at his watch. From behind him, a woman spoke and she wasn't the lovely French woman who announced gate changes; she was a rude beast with a penchant for causing agitation.

"I suppose that no matter where I go to get around you, you're just going to drift that way too." She yelled, the voice of an angry lioness. "Lazy traveler!"

Bill turned his head slightly to the left and when he did that he drifted that way too, "sorry."

"My God, pick a lane!" The dirty blonde with a husky figure said. She stormed past him with her Gucci rollaboard, a big Gucci hand bag and Gucci ladies pack. If they had a disco ball hanging from them, the bags couldn't have been any brighter. She had her hair all knotted up and tucked neatly against the back of her head. Her face was a soft cloud from a very good plastic surgeon.

"Got your overhead bin and under seat storage all set then." Bill said and shook his head at her. "Hope I can afford that surgery when I'm sixty." He got to the gate area and frowned.

A mob stood around the gate and a short line waited in the Sky Priority lane, first class. The devil's mistress who yelled at Bill earlier maneuvered her way around people with physical and verbal belches to get to the front of the line.

"They called first class!" She bumped a kid and then a man, "Why are all you people up here?" She nudged past two women who had parked themselves just to the side of the "Sky Priority Lane." She looked them over, "move or help!"

"Ladies and gentlemen, flight ninety-nine Paris to Atlanta is ready to board our Premium cabin." The gate agent said, "We're boarding the *premium cabin only* ... first class."

Bill sat down and people watched, but his wandering gaze was interrupted by the angry dirty blonde again.

"I don't care!" She shouted. "You're not changing my seat!" She yelled and then pulled her wheeled carryon up so that no one could get by. "Back off!" A man tried to get past her bag and she gave him an evil eye.

The passengers behind her gave out one exhaustive sigh.

"Change it back!" She snapped and looked at another agent who was busy at a screen. "You … you! You change my seat back! International first class and this is how you treat a Diamond medallion traveler, Diamond Medallion!" She focused on the agent. "My seat was a window seat with direct aisle access, not next to someone else … fix it!" She firmed up her grip on her luggage.

Bill laughed to himself. "Be nice to have a bed to lie down on for an eleven-hour flight."

"Idiots!" She let out, got her phone in hand and filmed them. "That's right! I got you on video, so don't try to screw me."

The agent handed her a ticket and his smile was far too wide to be real.

She looked at the ticket and shook her head. Then, she scanned her ticket and boarded.

Another exhaustive sigh came over the crowd that waited to board.

The last group was called. Bill got up and worked his way towards the group fifteen boarding area. No, there wasn't any group fifteen, but it felt like it when the very end of the boarding list was announced and you saw twenty people remaining and two-hundred boarded already. He was at the very back of the plane. He boarded mid-plane and glanced left at first class; there were seats within alcoves and drinks going around. "Pauper class for me," he turned, got his carryon turned and walked past rows of passengers. At the back, he fought for a space to put his carryon in and settled into his aisle seat. Three, three and three across, "Man, this is tight."

The woman next to him frowned. "Thanks for saying that … you think a middle seat is better?"

"Sorry," he said.

"The boarding door is closed now." The Flight attendant said. "Cross check please."

The plane was pushed back. A quick taxi and they were in the air in minutes. The flight attendants managed lunch quickly. Most of the passengers were caught up in their seat back videos. Bill checked the aisle and got up. He went to walk up the plane, but a flight attendant called to him.

"Sir, I'm sorry, but the lavatory for main cabin is at the back." She held her hand up to usher him that way.

Six hours later and just about everyone was asleep upright. Some turbulence jostled the plane and it teetered to the left and then to the right. He didn't sleep well on any flight. The control was out of your hands. Not even the most experienced pilot with the most advanced plane could un-ruffle turbulence. The clouds beneath them were dark, ominous. Anxiety pulsed through him in jolts. His eyes darted to the emergency exit, "in the event of an emergency, the nearest exit may be behind you." He turned back and looked the door over. Then, he reached for the plane's information card. "Just in case," he mumbled.

"BOOM!" The side of the plane dipped hard to the right.

Screams blew out of the few people who were awake. Other people woke to the noise and fought their senses which told them they were in trouble.

"Ladies and gentleman, the captain has turned on the seatbelt sign," then the lights flickered. "BOOM!" The plane pitched slightly nose down and then nosed back up.

Screams erupted!

"Jesus," The chewed-up lunch meat lurched up Bill's throat where it waited to be vomited.

"You think God's going to help right now?" The woman in the middle said.

"Ladies and gentleman, Captain Neuman here." Then, an abrupt *click* that the mic disconnected. The lights flickered and then brightened to their maximum.

"Capt. Newman here, we have an issue with our number two engine, right side of the aircraft." He clicked off.

The clicks jolted everyone's hearts.

The plane hummed and leveled out. "We can fly on one engine for some time folks." CLICK! "We're going to continue towards the eastern seaboard of the US." CLICK! "It'll take a little longer, but safety is paramount right now." CLICK! "Flight attendants, prepare the cabin." CLICK!

Flight services were over and you could only get up to pee or poop, now, on an emergency basis. Some people cried and things turned surreal. Flight attendants pulled life vests out and put them on. Passengers frantically searched the aisle for the flight attendants. Did they or should they get their life vest out? Some passengers pulled the red tab at the base of their seat, pulled their life vest out and when other people saw it, they did the same. Confusion reigned.

"Ladies and gentlemen, the cabin crew will assist you in the event you need a life preserver, please stop removing them, thank you." She said and then didn't let the mic button go. So, everyone overheard her say, "my God, we're not crashing yet ... oh damn it." CLICK!

Bill hesitated, because the plane was level and quiet. Why rush now? Though, he looked at his watch more times than he'd looked at it all year.

"Ladies and gentlemen," the captain said. "When the engine quit, it caused some damage to the control surfaces." CLICK!

Some moans and subtle cries could be heard. Fearing the worst without hearing it first was common on airplanes; there was only one place to land this far over the Atlantic, the water.

"Oh man," Bill said.

Passengers on the right side looked over each other at the wing.

"The damage to the control surfaces can be balanced out by using opposing control." CLICK. "However, the damaged wing is ..." A sigh came out, a worrying sigh that mothers make when they tell their young children, "No, I'm not buying you candy."

"We're looking at our options and we're on the phone with some experts about what to do." He said and there was no click this time. The background radio chatter came over the mic. "So, you're sure?" Then, the person on the other end said, "unfortunately Jim, find a spot, be sure that GPS and your coordinates are spot on. We'll get to …" CLICK!

Goose bumps leapt onto every living soul!

Bill leaned over the woman between him and the window seat. He looked at the dark clouds that swirled beneath them and mumbled, "The devil's stirring that brew."

She looked at him, "Really?"

The plane bounced and then the rear of the plane suddenly shifted one direction and then another; it was a car on a dirt road doing fishtails! People screamed! Bill sat back and his hands had a monster's grip on the seat armrest, a bare-knuckle grip.

There were two beeps and a flight attendant hurried to the back.

"Are we going to crash?" The woman in the middle asked. "Seriously, we must be miles from land." She tried to look over Bill. "Hello!" She looked for the flight attendant.

"BOOM!" The plane jerked to the left and some overhead bins burst open! Carryon's and coats and bags fell out! Screams erupted and some people got hit on the head.

"Ladies and gentlemen, so the final thing here is that, I'm sorry to say, but we are going to do a water landing." Now, fear vomited over every single person!

"Flight attendants prepare the cabin." CLICK! Now, they wanted you in a life preserver!

People in shock got up and tried to get their things. Other people pulled their life vest out and inflated them in the seat! Some bags fell from the overhead bins; they landed on people or fell in the aisle where they blocked it. The dirty blonde, from first class, rushed down the aisle with her large Gucci bag to the back of the plane. She lifted her legs high over a bag in the aisle and dragged her Gucci over it.

"Ma'am!" The flight attendant yelled, "Take your seat!"

"I know what happens when these things go down!" She half ran, half walked and looked older now in the bright light with heavy cheeks and strong lines around her mouth from fake laughs and forced smiles. Bitterness and fear were her new friends. She pushed past seats and ricocheted off of them!

"Ladies and gentlemen, remain seated!" The flight attendant shouted, "Remain seated if you want to survive!" Some people got their wits back and sat back down. The dirty blonde disappeared behind the last row into a bathroom and slammed the door shut.

One guy a row over popped his vest! "Damn thing's in the way!" He shouted.

The plane hummed, shook and rocked back and forth! Bill looked over the two passengers to his left and peered out the window. The ocean had white caps that were highlighted with every lightning strike! His heartbeat roared!

"My God," Bill said and realized at that very moment, they were going to crash in seconds. He sat back in his seat and looked straight ahead. Then …

Chapter 2: Open Ocean

WHAM! The plane slammed into the water, jolted up and the fuselage split open! People were ripped from their seats and thrown into the ocean! The plane bounced, hit again and broke into sections. The cockpit and first-class part of the fuselage went under in minutes! Faces looked up at the surface and bubbles drifted from their mouths; passengers fought with their seat belts and luggage drifted over them. At the rear of the aircraft, water rushed up the aisle; they were afloat, for now. People leapt from their seats, some with life preservers on and some without. People grabbed carry-ons and their personal things, then they naturally went to the front, but that section of the plane was gone. So, some people just dove into the water!

Thunder clapped around them, lightning flashed and heavy rain drops pelted them!

The plane lurched up and then dropped down; it might have believed that it was, now, a ship on the huge waves. The heavy rain covered Bill's eyes and he shook the droplets off only to have a hundred more cover his face, "get up, Bill … get up."

The woman in the middle seat punched his arm and tried to climb over him. "GET THE HELL UP!" She screamed at him, but he didn't feel any of it.

Then, she kneed his leg, "Move!" She climbed over him and the man climbed over him too.

He looked up and the cabin lights were off. The aisle and emergency lights flickered under the water. "Get up, Bill. GET THE HELL UP!" He pulled at his seatbelt and got up. "Help!" The cabin was nearly empty. Most of the passengers were in the water or swam towards a couple of life rafts that hung from the door behind the wing. He shook his head and wiped the rain from his face again. "The nearest exit may be behind you." He turned and a man was at the back door already.

The plane lurched and dipped. Water rose to the seat cushions! Bill looked at the overhead bin and wondered. Then, he looked down. "Life vest." He got the life vest from under his seat and the cabin tipped downwards which brought the tail section up. Quickly, he got his arms and legs through the loops, pulled the straps and tightened it. He looked at the overhead bin and went to open it, but stopped; "Bill, you … you gotta just go." He gripped the seat to stay himself.

The ocean lapped at his calves. "GO!" He shouted and made his way to the last exit door at the very rear of the plane. The door across from him was blocked with a couple of carts that must've come out when they crashed. The other door was open and a large yellow raft was tethered to the frame.

The dirty blonde pulled at the rope that held the raft to the plane.

"Wait for me!" Bill shouted at her.

"You untie us!" She shoved her Gucci bag to the other end of the raft.

A man bumped into Bill. "It's just us!" He was a heavy-set man with no neck and a shirt that had, "PARIS" across it with pictures of famous landmarks of France.

The plane lurched up and then the tail fell down. The ocean splashed into the raft and tried to claim it.

Bill looked at the cabin and thought. The only thing that kept them level must be the tail's wings. "Go, get on!"

The man pushed past with his rollaboard.

"You can't take that!" Bill yelled at him.

"I'm not leaving my souvenirs!" He tripped at the door and fell head first into the raft with his rollaboard right behind him.

The fuselage groaned; that was it. Bill went to step on, but stopped.

"Get on or get lost!" The dirty blonde shouted.

"C'mon buddy!" The man yelled.

The fuselage rolled up again with the waves and then the rear dipped as the wave passed.

Bill walked a few steps and looked at the seats, "Anyone there!" He waited and the ocean slammed against his legs. "ANYONE!" That *was* it. He had to go or go down with it. He rushed back to the door and the man's hands were busy trying to untie the tether that was under water. Bill got his fingers into the tab and a wave shifted the fuselage hard!

The wave threw Bill from the plane into the middle of the raft.

The man pulled at the tether and fought with it. "I ... it's not coming loose!"

Bill shouted. "Didn't you read the manual?"

The fuselage sank further and, now, the raft was being pulled under with it.

"No, who reads that stuff!" He slammed his fists on the tether. He slammed the water that crept over the tether and into the raft. The plane was taking the raft down!

"We're going to drown because of one idiot!" The dirty blonde shouted.

Bill turned to her and then turned to the man. Their end of the raft was partly under water. He had to move, "Bill, go … GO NOW!" He told himself, then leapt to the end where the raft was being firmly pulled under by the fuselage. The tail section was well on its way to the depths. Bill wiped the rain or tears of fear from his eyes, "Christ, almighty." He looked at the man and then the dirty blonde. "Hell with it." He turned back, slid off the end of the raft and went under.

Bill fanned his arms to get to the tabs. His vest wasn't inflated and fluttered like paper flaps as he swam down. He saw two bright yellow and red plastic tabs despite the blur of the salt water in his eyes. Beneath him was dark blue, the depths of a beast with its mouth *wide* open. He kicked his feet and moved closer and closer to the tabs. He got one tab and pulled it, nothing. He swung his feet down and against the floor of the door. Then, he got both hands on the tab as bubbles, his air, drifted past his eyes. He pulled and "POP!" the first tab unhooked. A part of the raft swooshed past him. He got his feet planted firmly again and had the last tab in hand. He pulled and "POP!" The tab tore the tether loose, the end of the raft screamed, "FREEDOM!" The raft swooshed up and shoved Bill's head into the top of the aluminum door frame, "crack!" A trail of blood seeped from gash to his head into the water.

His eyes were fixed on the tail end of the plane as it sank into the beast's mouth. His heart beat hard against his chest and yelled at him, "AIR!" He swallowed a gulp of ocean water, kicked and then looked at the bubbles, the way up! He pushed with his arms and his head popped out of the water! "AH!"

A wave lifted him up to its peak where the white cap splashed his face. "HELP!"

"There he is!" The man shouted and threw a life preserver to him. "Get it!"

Bill pulled the tab on his life vest! The vest blew up and helped him float. He threw his arms out and swam for the doughnut. "Got it!"

The man dragged him to the raft and the dirty blonde sneered.

The man pulled Bill from the beast's mouth. "Got you, I got you!"

She looked at them and the size of the raft, "big enough, I guess." She clutched her Gucci bag, "it's water proof."

"Thanks," Bill said and turned to sit upright. He looked around them. "There's got to be others."

Thunder clapped and lightning bolted over them! Thousands of rain droplets poured all over.

"You see anyone?" He looked at the man and then the dirty blonde. "Anyone?"

She didn't look. The man looked around them just as a wave lifted them to its crest and then dropped them for the next wave.

"No," the man said and got his bag in hand. "I ... maybe they drifted away."

"Maybe," the woman said and didn't take her eyes from her things.

The raft rolled with the waves and bucked when the wind caught it.

Bill looked around again and there wasn't anything that looked like part of the plane, a raft or people that he could see. "Jesus," he wiped his brow. "They can't all have gone under." He sat up, but fear pushed him back down; he couldn't bring himself to look at the depths again.

"You mean drowned." The dirty blonde said and looked pale, tired. Her hair was a matted bird's nest that hadn't seen a chick in years.

Bill and her locked eyes; despite being soaked with cold Atlantic Ocean water, his face warmed.

"Maybe they got to some other rafts?" The man said. "I'm Martin."

Bill broke his gaze and swallowed some of the salt water that was left in his mouth. "Bill," he rubbed his head and spat. Blood slithered down his forehead to his cheek.

"You got a nasty cut to your head." Martin said.

Bill felt the cut and looked at his fingers. Some blood swished around on his fingertips before it spilled into the raft.

The dirty blonde made a squeamish look and then fanned her nose. She pulled the zipper to her bag open, dug her hand in and searched inside.

"Should be a first aid kit in here," Bill got up and looked around. He half-slid, half-crawled to the front of the raft where the dirty blonde clutched her big bag.

The downpour was over, but the rain was not. Each wave took the raft up and then down in deep swells.

"Don't get any blood on me." She slid away from him.

He eyed her and then lifted a plastic lid to a big orange box. "Here we go." There was a flare gun with flares, some towels, a radio, and life preservers. "Some food and water in here."

"I'm not thirsty." Martin said.

The dirty blonde looked at him and shook her head.

The dark clouds grew gray and the lightning took its terror further away.

Bill got some tape and a gauze bandage out. He fought to keep his balance while taping the gauze to his head.

Martin leaned up and reached out to him. "Let me," he took the gauze and wrapped it around Bill's forehead. Then, he tore it and knotted it behind Bill's head.

"Thanks," Bill nodded at him. And then looked his life vest over. He pulled a tab and it deflated.

The dirty blonde pulled out a flowered blue poncho. She set her bag to the side and put it on.

"What's your name?" Martin looked at the dirty blonde and smiled heartily.

She rolled her eyes and then sighed, "Claire."

"That's a nice name." Martin dug around in his bag. "My fiancé' …" His face told the truth while his mouth finished the lie. "Her name is Sherry."

"I'm sorry, you must be in shock. We just crashed and are adrift in the middle of the ocean," Claire said and looked around. "She seated with you?"

Bill bowed his head and shook it. Then, he looked up. "Really lady?"

Martin tried to smile, "no … she, we're not together anymore."

"Fiancé, but you're not together anymore." Claire pretended to look in her bag and mumbled, "okay, one crazy person identified."

Bill looked at her, squinted and then turned to Martin. "So, you broke up."

"Yeah, well … no." He frowned. "She left me."

Claire mumbled, "No surprise there."

Bill looked at her and his face warmed again.

"But, you know," Martin said and pulled a metal Eiffel Tower souvenir from his bag; it was about ten inches tall. "Got her an Eiffel Tower … see if that doesn't bring her round."

"You're an idiot." Claire said, got to her knees and crawled over to Martin.

"What?" Martin asked.

"What the hell's your deal lady?" Bill wanted to throw her back in the plane.

She crawled to Martin. "She left you and you got her something; you're an idiot." She grabbed the Eiffel Tower and threw it into the water. "Grow a pair already."

"Hey!" Bill pushed her back. "Don't do that."

"It's done and don't touch me!" She threw her poncho up to block Bill's hands, "just don't."

"You don't get to act like that!" Bill shouted.

"It's okay, really." Martin dug around in his bag.

"See, he's an idiot." She shook her head, feigned a laugh, and then went back to her bag.

"Stop calling him that." Bill's face was hot and his cold cheeks were an ashen red.

"I've got another one in case something happened to one of them." Martin smiled and felt some sense of pride that he thought ahead. "I mean, one was for me, but I have my memories and pictures." He smiled brightly, "I've got all kinds of souvenirs, nice ones."

"My God, how do you people function in life?" Claire got on her knees and steadied herself. The next wave lifted them high. "Idiot, no wonder she left you!"

"Hey! Sit down and stop picking at him." Bill said and felt dizzy, not from the waves alone, but from his concussion.

"You do not tell me what to do, ever!" She crawled back to Martin. The wave peaked under the raft and then dropped them! She fell on Martin!

"Get off of me!" Martin drew the Eiffel Tower to his chest.

She grabbed the Eiffel Tower and the fight was on! She pulled, he pulled, she jerked and he jerked the other way!

"Stop it!" Bill yelled, "Just stop already before one of you goes over!"

Martin turned and, with his weight, he jerked the Eiffel Tower from her hands and stabbed the raft. "POP!"

"No way," Bill looked at Martin, looked at her, and then looked at the hole. "You're an *idiot*, lady."

"Idiot!" She slapped him. "He's such an idiot!" She pointed, "he poked the hole in the raft!"

Bill shoved her to the side and that section of the raft deflated quickly.

Claire crawled to her big bag at the other end.

Martin quickly put his Eiffel Tower in his bag, put his bag in his lap and wrapped his arms around it tightly.

"Martin," Bill got a rope from the survival pack, tied it around him and then tied it to a hook on the raft. He pointed at Martin's bag, "that bag float?"

"I'm not letting it go!" The raft's rim gave out and Martin went legs up and over backwards into the water with the rollaboard.

"Martin!" Bill pushed through the water that was all over the raft. "MARTIN!"

"He's never gonna let that bag go. Just like he can't let her …" Claire waved bye to Martin.

"Shut up!" Bill dove in after him.

Martin sank with the rollaboard clutched to his chest. Bill's hands shot out and then pulled back! He swam to Martin, but Martin went deeper and sank fast.

Martin looked at Bill and held tightly to his bag. The weight of the souvenirs in the rollaboard wasn't as heavy as his heart, but it was heavy enough to sink him.

Bill saw the vast darkness behind Martin; the beast opened its mouth again and Bill stopped, any deeper and he would drown too.

Chapter 3: Adrift and Bigger is Better

Bill didn't want to watch that poor man anymore, but he couldn't turn his eyes away. Hope, Bill hoped that at that last minute, Martin would hear, "you're going to die; do something different." But Martin didn't and he faded into the beast's dark blue mouth, gone forever with his souvenirs.

Bill's mind said, "You're going to die; do something different!" He shook, gulped a mouthful of saltwater and then headed back to the surface.

The raft was a big yellow blob and it still floated … partially. He pulled himself onto it and crawled to the center.

"See," she rolled her eyes. "My bag floats."

Bill was so angry, so ready to push her in that he had to look away. He looked around and hoped again that he would see someone, anyone floating nearby or swimming and crying out for help. He spat and turned to her. "I'm no idiot and it's just you and me now."

"Are you threatening me?" She looked around.

"Yeah, why?" He spat again. "You gonna call for help here." His voice roared, "In the middle of the Atlantic Ocean!" He went to stand and sank into the yellow blob. His legs quickly jostled around to get up and out. Then, he realized he had to stay where he was. He really wanted to slap her, hard.

She wiped her eyes. "I'm in shock, okay."

"A man just died over the Eiffel Tower!" He snapped, got the rope untied from the raft and tied it to the orange safety trunk.

She sniffled and looked away, "a souvenir." She mumbled.

The rain's tiny droplets cooled his face and the horrendous thunderclouds thinned.

"Christ man, he died over his souvenirs." He shook his head and felt the tug of the trunk with the flares, first aid, water and food.

That night, his temper eased. The raft was a kind of a kid's plastic pool that floated on the ocean, but had water in it. He looked around and wondered when the raft might give out and feed the beast beneath them. His anxiety climbed and he mumbled, "hate having nothing under me … blue abyss." He fought back a surge of emotion that brought small tears to his eyes.

She rested against her bag and looked at the stars. Then, she swallowed hard. "I need some water."

He shook his head. Then, he pulled the survival trunk to him and got a packet of water. "There's only six water packs in here and some granola bars." He got a water pack in hand and wanted to bean her with it. But, he wasn't a mean person. So, he edged up and tossed it to her.

The sack landed just near her feet. She sat up and got it, "thanks."

"Wow, bet that hurt." He pursed his lips.

"Look, I'm not a bad person." She huffed. "We crashed and …" Her eyes welled up. "I'm here, stranded."

"We're stranded." He said and made sure the rope was tied tightly to the survival trunk.

She fought with the packet and pulled at it. Then, she looked at Bill. "Why didn't you open it for me?"

"Just tear it from the corner." He huffed.

She held it up. "You do it."

"Wow, you have no manners." He crawled over, pulled the edge and opened it. "You're welcome."

She sighed hard, "okay then."

The thunder clouds were gone and the storm swept everything from the sky and water. The stars shined against the solid darkness of space.

"Should try to rest," he said and pulled the pack under his head.

"How?"

"Any way you can," he lay back with his body half floating in the water that licked his sides.

She scoffed, looked around and then tried to get comfortable with her big suitcase behind her.

The raft slowly drifted on the backs of easy waves into the late night and wees hours of the morning. A few birds that trailed the storm hung in the air just above them. The moon's glow glided up and over each wave along with them in a peaceful dance.

Morning, the sun crested the horizon and orange lines strode across an easy blue sky that chased the nighttime away. A yawn overtook Bill before he could catch his breath. Then, he sat up and studied his legs, which half hung above and below a big puddle of water. Was it real? He lifted his leg and the water from his jeans dripped off "damn the luck." He turned and Claire had her knees up to her chest.

Her arms were crossed and her head cocked to one side where her poncho bunched up and made a kind of air pillow. She yawned and turned to get comfortable, "AH!" She let out and scrambled to get to her feet.

"Don't try to stand!" He shouted at her.

"What!" Her legs pushed her up and then they sank right into the raft! "I'm sinking!"

"Sit down!" He shouted and waved his hands at her, "JUST SIT!"

She plopped down and a splash of water blew out from her backside. Her bag drifted a foot or so away. She quickly turned, grabbed it and pulled it to her. "So, it's not a dream."

"Nope," he looked around and licked his dried lips. "Need some water," he got the rope and pulled the survival trunk to him, got a water pack and opened it. He got through half when he suddenly stopped. "Oh man," he muttered.

"What?" She tried to sit up. "What did you say?"

"Got to conserve our water," he looked around them.

"Don't look at me ... you have it all." She worked at her hair to pull it back.

He reached in and got two packs. "I gave you one already?"

"Yes," she pulled her poncho head piece back and down. "But I don't have anywhere to put it."

"Too many souvenirs?" He grinned.

She sneered, "hardly."

"The pilot told them we were in trouble." He got the packet of water sealed and put it with the rest of the gear.

She sat up the best she could with her back against her bag. "Thousands of miles of ocean."

"We have the flares and the radio." He looked at the trunk and there it was, "says this is a rescue radio beacon".

"AM or FM?"

"Think it's just for signaling rescuers." He looked it over and then looked around the raft.

"What are you looking for?" She wiped the salt ridden sweat from her forehead.

"The oars," he edged up and crawled a few feet.

"What do they look like?" She pushed out.

"Oars," he said and shook his head.

"Yes, you said that, but that's not helpful." She sat up. "Oh look, I don't want to be here either!"

He huffed, "a stick with a flat wide piece at the end of the stick."

She looked around and then pointed, "There, that's one."

He crawled over, "great."

"I saw one float away when you went …" She covered her mouth.

"For Martin?"

"Yes," she turned away.

"So, just one oar then." He looked around some more and then crawled back to where he rested. The corner of the raft still had some air in it. "We can't stay in the water for long."

"No, we can't." She touched her face, "it's bad for the skin."

"Uh-huh," he looked around and got up on the edge of the raft that floated. "We could be out here for days."

"You really think so?" She caught her breath. "Are you a fisherman?"

He chuckled. "No, I work in tech."

"Oh," she squinted when she thought. "So, then how can you tell how long it'll take to get rescued?"

"Thousands of miles of ocean and the storm carried us away from where we crashed." He looked up.

"I see …a jack of all trades and master of none." She wiped the sleep from her eyes.

"Don't say that to me." He sighed hard, "Look, we might die out here."

"What is it with men that they are always doom and gloom, doom and gloom … just the worst." She turned away.

"Wow, okay." He looked at the sun and then looked west. "Sun rises in the east."

"You know that too." She scoffed. "And how does that help us?"

"Gives us a direction to go," he got the oar and paddled. "We'll head west. We were half way through our trip when we had trouble."

"You mean crashed." She pulled her poncho off in a fury. "You mean crash!" She flung it. "Now, you want to act like you have some hope?" She shook her head hard. "I'm so glad I'm divorced."

"Why don't you just calm down ... okay?" He drew the oar back and then out, then back. "Just chill."

She tried to smile, turned and then rested on her luggage. "My ex-husband used to say that ... just calm down, just calm down."

He looked up and rolled his eyes.

The sun climbed up from the east and followed them across the ocean to see where they were going to go or get to by the end of its day. The ocean was calmer and the waves rolled under them in gentle rises and falls.

Bill got a snack bar out and tossed it to her. Claire was in tears and rambled on about nothing.

"This is life." She mumbled, "life with things and people you stay away from and then there's a curse."

"Have some water." He said.

"Oh, wouldn't you like that." She slammed her hands down and water splashed up.

"Not saltwater lady, drink some water from the packet." He rolled his eyes again.

"Don't tell me what to do!" She slammed her hands down again. "Don't tell me!"

"You need to have some water!" He looked down and then back at her. "Would you please have a drink?" He sighed, "It will help you."

"I will have a drink when I want too!" She yelled. Then, she got the pack of water and drank.

He looked away, better to focus in a different direction than to give her any more life. "Drink whatever, but you may want to think about making it last."

"Why?" She snapped. "Does it mean I'll have to put up with you longer?" She slammed the pack down and ocean water splashed up to her face. "I pay to fly better airlines." She looked up. "I pay for first class so I can separate myself from this kind of crap!" Her eyes welled up.

"From a plane crash?" His mouth fell open and then he hesitated. Why wind her up? His mouth closed and he oared the yellow blob west.

"Oh, shut up!" She shouted.

A big yellow blob in the water would be easy to spot as long as it didn't sink. His heart missed a beat. That yellow blob under him was all that kept him calm.

"We're adrift, floating above the abyss!" She let out and pressed both her hands against her head.

"The raft's big and it's yellow, very easy to see." He drew back, lifted and dug the oar in, repeat.

Her head slowly rose until she looked up again. "I don't see any planes." Her head turned this way and that way; her cheeks burned red. "I don't see any damn planes!" She slammed her hands over and over in the water. "I don't see any damn … plane that are looking for this big damn … yellow blob in the water!"

"No, not yet," he said and made a heavy sigh.

"Just shut up!" She threw the water pouch at him. "God, this is why I was in first class! So, I wouldn't have to be in the company of people … like you!" She pulled her poncho over her head and cried. "I hate people." She muttered, "middle class people who always have something smart to say, but no money to make what they say matter."

He tasted the urge, the sweetness of saying something that would annoy her further. Then, he drew in a deep breath and … she's in shock he thought. He sighed and drew the oar back, then up, dug in and repeated it.

They drifted with the current that moved them far more than Bill's oaring. He looked at his shoes and jeans. His feet had been under water for hours. Claire had sandals he thought.

"Hey," he said and looked at her legs. "Hey!"

"What!" She snapped and sat up.

"You need to find a way to get your legs up." He jerked his shoes off and set them aside with his socks. His feet were a pasty white and warped.

"Oh, you are so disgusting." She tightened her legs so that they were locked together. "Just try it."

"Oh my God, really?" He shook his head and his mouth hung open. "Your legs have been under water for hours with no air."

"No shit." She snapped.

"Maybe, you should take your attitude and put it in your big ass trunk. Then, put it under your legs to get them air for your frigging health!" He slammed his hand on the water, "moron."

"You don't get to call me that!" She kicked at the water in a fit and then froze. Something caught her eye to the side of them. "What's that?" Her sun-dried face paled and her hand went up slowly to point.

"What?" He turned. A shark fin rose up and coasted along the water just a few feet from them. His heart missed a bunch of beats, "No way."

"Hit it," she said and smacked her hand on the water. "Hit it with the oar!" She slammed her hand on the water. "You!" She screamed, "Hit that God damned shark!"

The fin slowly sank into the glistening edge of the water.

"The more noise you make, the more attractive we are!" His face burned and he held the oar up. "So, just …" and he spelled out the word, "S.T.H.U already!"

"What does that mean?" She looked all around them and then screamed bloody murder. "AH!" She jumped and drew her legs up.

"Now, she brings her legs up." His heart beat at a fevered pace.

"It just went under me!" She gripped her luggage and looked around her butt. "Do they bite?"

38

He turned to her and shook his head. "Only if you keep *screaming*." He turned and tried to bring his feet up against him. "Yell some more."

She squinted and eyed him, "You people are so terrible."

"My people?" He turned away and was puzzled.

Something bumped the raft and the yellow blob shifted with the force of something under it.

He figured that the shark, at some point, was going to take a bite out of the raft. "He's teasing the raft."

"Like you know, Mr. Jack of all trades." She kicked her foot at him. "I don't like you."

Goose bumps bubbled up all over him. "Don't call me that!"

"Master of nothing," she flipped him off.

"You are such a hateful person." He made like he was going to hit her with the oar when her eyes got big and her middle finger pointed behind him.

"It's ..." She gulped and her throat popped out.

"What?" Then, his heart pleaded with him not to look, so he leapt!

The shark's nose came up first and then there were rows of pristine white, jagged teeth that ripped the yellow blob's punctured end to shreds! The shark was big, better than ten or twelve feet. It jerked its head back and forth to tear a piece of yellow meat free! That end of the raft jerked this way and that way. Then, the shark jerked back and the raft jerked towards it!

"Christ!" Bill crawled closer to her. "That end was already out of air."

"Don't come near me!" She waved her hands at him.

"Where the hell am I going to go!" He stopped and had the oar at his feet.

The shark clamped down, thrashed, and its teeth slashed the raft.

"He wants you!" She yelled, "Don't bring him here." She pointed.

The shark dipped its head and was gone. Some suds stirred and little swirls of water went on for few moments after his big tail whipped them up.

"Now, I know!" She yelped. "Didn't you see that movie, Paws?"

He looked her over and rolled his eye, "*Jaws*." The survival trunk slid into the water, just near the side of the torn raft. He looked at the rope and followed it up to his waist where it was wrapped twice around him and knotted. The shark's fin came up on the other side and their eyes locked on it. "No, no, no, no." He pulled at the knot, but the salt water made it shrink and firmed up the knot. The only way to get it off was to bite through the rope. His fingers worked at the knot in a frenzy! "No, no, no!"

"Stop making so much noise, he'll attack." She said calmly and looked in her luggage for something. "Gosh, like one of those westerns on TV." The sun was right over them, "high noon."

Bill looked to the right and no fin; then he snapped his head the other way and no fin. He looked around them with a one-eighty that way and a one-eighty this way. "Where is he?"

"Jack of all trades …" She muttered, "One bite and you know it's a he?" She shook her head.

"Shut up!" He shouted at her.

Then, there was a ferocious splash! The shark sank its teeth into the survival trunk and swam off! He took up the slack in the rope as he swam further and further away!

Bill's fingers pulled and picked at the knot! Then, he felt a tug. "Oh God … no."

"That shark is going to pull you in." She said. "I wouldn't want to be you."

"No!" The rope was taught. The shark dragged Bill towards the flat edge of the raft. He flipped around and got his feet jammed into the raft, but the shark pulled and Bill sank down to his waist! "Help me!"

She pulled something from her bag. "Here!" She had a pair of fingernail scissors. "HERE!" She tossed them over and they fell into the water by him. He scurried to get them.

The shark jerked its head and yanked Bill from his little pocket of safety.

"Help!" The shark thrashed and swam deeper with Bill in tow. Once Bill was at the edge of the raft, he'd go right in and under. His heart raced and his muscles twitched with fear! "HELP!"

Chapter 4: ATOLL

She looked around for something to do, something to help with. "What … what do you want me to do?"

He looked at her and was dumbfounded. He was on his way, head first, into the ocean for dinner and nothing was going to save him. Then, there was a huge splash!

The shark shot out of the water with the trunk in its mouth and an orca shot up right next to him! The orca opened its mouth wide and bit down on the shark's stomach! The shark's mouth opened up to scream out in pain, but the trunk was in the way. They both hit the water and a wave blew up and over Bill and Claire!

Water dripped down their faces and they both stared on in horror and amazement. Just then, the trunk popped up and drifted just a few feet from the edge of the torn raft.

Claire looked at it. "You should get that." She pointed at it. "We need that stuff and … do you still have my clippers?"

He slowly turned to her and his mouth had had enough, "*shut* the hell up." He fell back against the raft and his body floated in inches deep water held up by their yellow blob. He got the trunk on the raft and then got the rope untied from him.

"Rude, you people are so …" She huffed and returned to rummaging through her bag.

He closed his eyes, "thank you God, bigger *is* better."

The sun set was beautiful and the ocean current carried them further away from the crash site. Bill rested from mental exhaustion and Claire tried to do her makeup and hair. The lite waves slowly rolled under the raft and massaged Bill's wet legs and back.

Bill got a drink of water and put the pack under his legs to keep them up and out of the water for the time being.

The sun wasn't kind and with the salt air, their skin began to dry out, burn.

Her lips and cheeks were a harsh reddish-brown. She dabbed some moisturizer on and got her vanity mirror steadied on her bag. The rouge really brought out her dry skin and her lips had tiny cracks. She got some water and shook the pack. "God, it's nearly empty." She looked at her side and then her other side. "I don't suppose you have any water left."

He sighed, "For me."

"So, what am I supposed to do?" She got the poncho and fluffed it up, then put it over her head so that it was like a tent over her. "Don't your people …" She caught her breath.

"My people what?" He turned to her. "What's your deal?"

She squinted, "middle class people are good givers."

He chuckled, "wow, you're a piece of work." His head fell lazily back against the half-inflated part of the raft. "So, just how rich are you?" He rubbed the cut on his head and cringed.

She threw the empty water pack at him, but the wind caught it and it flew up.

"That's great, more litter in the ocean." He pulled the life vest over his face and off.

"I'm sure *your* people will do something to clean it up." She huffed.

"My people," he got the half-used water pack from his side, sat up and tossed it to her. "That's it."

She got it and then something caught her eye. "What's that?"

"If it's another shark, just keep talking." He said.

She sneered, opened the water and took a drink.

"Maybe you're seeing things … drink the water."

"I'm not seeing things." She leaned up. "It's something."

"Really?" He sat up. "Oh damn." Barely enough to break the water's edge, "might be an island …maybe an atoll."

"Atoll?"

"It's made of coral, sand." He looked at her. "Don't even say it."

A half-hearted smile crossed her face. "Alright, are you going to oar us there?" She pushed her hair back.

He edged up as much as he could before his knees sank into the raft. "Yeah, why not." He got the oar and paddled. "Not much sun left."

"Does it matter?"

"Yeah, if you want to get to that island." He moved to the other side.

"Why do you keep moving?" She shook her head in disapproval. "You're wasting time."

"Because, I need a good spot to oar from." He brought his knees under him. "Unless you want to."

"Boating, planes, sharks, is there anything …" She stopped.

He turned and they locked eyes, "you want me to oar, then you need to find something else to do with your mouth." His arm went up with the oar, dug in and drew back.

"Fine," she looked around her. "Still don't have my clippers that I lent you."

He bowed his head and shook it. Then, he looked ahead. There *was* an island and, if he was lucky, she could go live on the other side of it.

"So, what does it mean to work in tech?" She looked her nails over.

He looked back, "huh?"

"Tech, that's what you said you do." She fanned herself.

"I work in computers." The oar sank in, drew back and then came out of the water.

"That's vague." She quipped.

He stopped and turned to her. "I network multiple PC's for end users in small business with no more than fifty employees so that they can work together on documents and spreadsheets via the cloud."

She raised a brow. "So, you work in tech."

He huffed and returned to oaring. There was more of the island. "It is an island."

"Good, have to see where I'll stay." She put her legs on her luggage. "My skin is screaming for help."

He mumbled, "I'm screaming for help too."

"What?" She snapped. "What did you say?" She sat up and nearly toppled over.

"Nothing," he drew the oar back and felt the sting of salt and sun on his forearms. "I wonder if anyone else survived."

She sighed, "You have the trunk."

"That's not the only trunk for that many people." He slapped the oar against the water and a spray of it went towards her.

"Ah!" She let out as the water splashed her, "so immature."

"So, like my people." He laughed to himself.

By that evening, the island was closer, but not enough for them to hop out.

"Why don't you tie the rope to the raft and swim to the island?" She looked around. "There are no more fins."

"Yeah, right." He turned to her. "Why don't you?"

She scoffed, "I'm … I don't know how to swim."

His eyes rolled twice over. "You better hope this raft floats all the way there then."

"Or what?"

"I'm not a lifeguard." He turned to her and a sly smile grew.

"But I thought you had so many trades." She made a funny face at him.

He turned back and the sun was in his face. The island was larger now, closer, but so was darkness. "Whatever," he said and oared on.

By dusk, they were within a mile or so of the island. Bill felt his anxiety climb, but the temptation was there to look over the side of the raft and see if there was dark blue or sand beneath the waves. He swallowed hard, got his nerves to calm down a little and edged up to the side of the raft.

"What are you doing?" She asked. "You're going to take my advice?"

"What advice is that?" He edged closer to the side of the raft that still had some air in it.

"Go in and pull us to the island." She smacked her hand on the water. "Go!" She smiled, "don't be afraid."

He jumped, "Don't!" His legs trembled and he locked eyes with her again. "Just don't." He turned and the raft's side gave out! "Ah!" He fell over and a splash of water lapped over the side of the raft.

"You don't have the rope!" She looked around her. "You!" She shouted. "Hey, you … tech guy!"

Bill flapped his arms around and pulled at the yellow blob. His feet kicked at the water and his fingers pulled to get him back on the raft, but he pulled the deflated raft under as he pulled it to him. "Do something!"

"Like what?" She crawled to the rope, got her fingers on it and tossed it to him. "Take the rope."

"God, you're useless!" He dragged himself back onto the yellow blob, but it was apparent that the raft was losing its last bit of life. His breaths shot in and out! "You …"

"Me what?" She looked at the island. "I threw you the rope."

"Yeah, to pull you along!" He yelled at her. "You didn't do it to save me."

"I can't swim." She turned away.

"The raft is done for." He looked at the sides and they were caving in.

"What?" Her attention changed and she looked at the yellow blob that was half sunk. "No, no it can't sink!" She got her big bag tight against her.

"It is sinking." He pulled the trunk to him. "Been better to drag it onto the beach."

"You …" She muttered. "You did this!"

"What?"

"You did it on purpose!" She slammed her hands on her bag. "You know I can't swim!" Her lightly burned cheeks turned dark rouge. "You people, just can't stand us."

"Stand who, you maniac!" His fist tightened and a surge of anger flowed through him like a lava flow in a volcano. The rope to the trunk was there at his feet. "You know what, maybe you're right … my people *can't* stand you!" He got the rope in hand, tied it off to a hook on the raft and dove in the

48

water. "I hate deep water!" But, it wasn't that deep. His heart beat so fast that the thumps vibrated the water around him. He looked down and then up, "okay, okay." He closed his eyes and then pushed up, "just do it." With the rope in hand, he swam towards the island. A few strokes later, he knew that he had to tie the rope off to himself. He treaded water, got the rope around his waist and looked for her. The yellow blob was too big, too wide to see her at the back of it. "Hope she goes in." He fought the urge to smile.

"We're not moving very much!" She yelled.

"You bit …!" A wave popped up and splashed his mouth. He spat it out, got his breath and then swam off.

The sun sizzled as it sank into the ocean at the end of the earth. Darkness chased the light away and took over until the moon shined on them.

"Can't see the bottom anyways, too dark." He swam slowly and didn't want to splash or slam his hands into the water. A shark might come. Then, his foot hit something on the down stroke, "Ah!"

"We there yet?" She let out.

He jerked his feet up and looked at the raft. "Should swim under and hit her butt." A smile pulled his chap lips apart and a little pain snapped him to. What was it his foot touched? The island was a hundred feet or more away and the water rolled over itself and crashed on the beach. His anxiety made him shiver. He reached down and felt around, nothing. Finally, he gave in and lowered his foot. "Oh, wow." It was the ocean floor. He pushed ahead and, now, got his footing on the sandy sea floor.

Waves pushed past him and crashed ahead of him.

"Hey!" She yelled. "It's … um, the raft is sinking; it's sinking!"

"Water's not that deep." He was waist deep.

"Help!" She yelled and fell in. "HELP!"

Bill pulled at the raft and got turned around, "damn her." She was out there and he'd have to work his way around the raft to get to her, "never, ever go under a boat." He looked at the blob, "especially one that's sinking."

"HELP!" She went under.

He shoved the trunk towards the beachhead and swam to her.

She flung her arms and legs in the water like it was a prize fight and she wasn't going down! "HELP ME!" Ocean water filled her mouth when she went under again and it filled her nostrils! She spat and choked on the salt water.

"I'm coming!" He saw her shadow flailing and fighting to stay afloat. "Just clam down!"

"You're trying to drown me!" She slammed her hands and then the ocean pulled her under!

He went under and the half-moon's glow was enough to see her. Once he got her in hand, he swam up and broke the surface. "CALM DOWN!"

She mumbled and choked on the water, "trying to kill me … kill my son."

"What?" He pulled her around the raft and then was able to stand. "Calm down, you're going to be alright … just stand up!" Even though he couldn't stand her, he wasn't going to just let her drown.

A large wave snuck up behind them, rolled over them and pushed them under!

"Da …" Bill said and then his mouth was full of water, only bubbles came out.

The wave slammed her down onto some coral and it cut her leg. The wave crashed and they were pulled back up.

"I'm done." She muttered.

"No, you're not …" he spat. "You're not done." His legs, painful as they were, marched onwards to the beach. They crawled up and lay breathless on the sand, "not done, not yet."

Two whispered words eased their way through her chapped lips, "Kill me."

He shook his head and passed out.

Early in the darkness of that next morning, Bill opened his eyes and ears. The waves gently crashed against the beach, a breeze rattled the palm fronds on the coconut trees and the sight of thousands of stars across a dark sky brightened his eyes. "Beautiful."

Morning, Claire sat up and licked her sunburned lips; her tongue passed over each crack and stung. Everything was a blur and she turned this way and that way to get her bearings. "Oh, thank God … it was a dream, a very bad dream." She sat up and then felt her leg, "ouch."

Bill was a few feet from her and lay still on the barren sand.

She thought for a moment and rubbed her temples, "Mark?" Then, the blurriness faded and the yellow blob lay before her. "Ah!" She screamed for a few seconds and then threw her hands up! "No!"

Bill jumped and then got up. "Damn!" Dazed from a lack of water and his head injury, he didn't put his hands out and fell over his own two feet, face first into the sand. "God, what …"

"You!" She turned on her side and tried to get up, but her leg gave out. "Owe!" She ran her hand down her leg and then she felt the cut, the gash to her thigh. "You cut me!"

He got his bearings. "I didn't cut you." His eyes did double rolls. "You hit something in the water."

She pursed her lips. "Right, when you sank the raft and tried to drown me."

He knew now where he was and what had happened. His feet got themselves right and he stood. "You didn't drown because I saved you."
"Oh, right … that's it." She was squeamish and glanced at her the rip in her capris. "Well, these LaChance capris are ruined, there's your thanks." She looked closer. "There's blood all over!"

"Calm down, I'm sure the salt water helped to keep your cut clean." He pulled at the rope and it was very heavy. "Going to get the trunk."

"Uh-huh," she scoffed. "And where are we Mr. Know it all?" She looked around. "My Gucci!" She fought to get up. "Where's my Gucci rollaboard!"

He stopped and looked down. "Bill, my name is Bill."

She huffed, "Bill … where's my Gucci rollaboard?"

"I don't know." He walked off.

She mumbled, "Well then what good are you."

His teeth ground together. His hands pulled and the yellow blob floated onto the sand where it dug in its heels. The trunk bobbed just a few feet away from the raft. "There it is." He got the trunk. Her Gucci bag was on the beach. "Your dumb bag is right there." He got the first aid. went to her and knelt. "Well?"

"Well what?" She put her hand over the rip in her capris. The cut was higher on her thigh then she realized, a little too high for a stranger to put cream.

"You want me to bandage it or not?" He got some iodine and took the cap off.

"A doctor too," she inched away.

"Look, knock it off or you can fend for yourself." He reached for the tear in her capris.

She smacked his hands. "I'll do it!" She snatched the iodine from him. "Let's not add rape to your list of trades."

"Lady, if I was going to die and had one wish …"

"Shut up!" She tipped the bottle over and the iodine splashed on her cut; it burned! "AH!"

"It burns." He chuckled.

"You knew that!" She threw the bottle.

"Don't!" He got up and ran to it, but the last bit trickled out before he could get the cap on. "Damn, it's all gone!"

She held her hand to her leg. "You should have told me it burned."

He drew in a deep breath. "Look, seriously, you need to get a frigging grip. That was the only way to kill an infection and now it's gone."

She came to her senses and sighed. "It's your fault."

"What!" He got to his feet and looked her up and down. "How do you make that out?"

She squirmed and her face reddened. "You didn't say it would burn. You didn't say it."

"Wow, really?" He went back to the trunk and looked through the first aid kit. There was a small tube of antibiotic salve. "Okay," he walked over to her and sat down. "This is antibiotic salve. You put a little bit in your cut and then cover your cut with this." He held up the gauze bandage and tape. "You can do it your damn self." He grabbed her hand.

"Let go of me!" She tried to pull back, but he was too strong. "LET GO!"

He squirted some salve onto her hand. "There," he let go. "So, you don't screw up anything else." He went back to the first aid kit and put it in.

"Wretched beast!" She shouted and then looked at her hand.

"Yep," he drank some water.

She looked on and licked her lips. "Water?"

"You used yours." He drank up and then shook it. "Here," he threw it at her, but didn't seal it up.

She fell onto her side to catch it. "Hey!" She reached out, got the pack, but some of the water dripped out and that's when she looked at him with a burning stare. "See, I was right. You people feel wronged and so you take it out on others."

"What are you talking about?" He touched the cut on his head and cringed.

"It's never your fault that you don't have a job or can't pay your bills." She slammed the water packet on the sand. "I hate you!" She threw the water packet at him.

"Okay," he got up and walked off. "Time for a break."

Besides the sunburn, her face was on fire. Her fists were clenched and she was ready for a fight. "Jack of nothing!"

He stopped, "go to hell lady." Then, he looked at the center of the island, walked up the sand bank and disappeared into the coconut trees, sea grape trees and sand brush, the jungle.

Her face cooled and she looked around. "Terrible, terrible … why I even bothered to let him pull me on land." She looked at the salve on her hand and sniffed it. "Terrible people," she got the tear in her capris open and smeared it on her cut. "Ah!"

He barely heard her yelp and pressed into the jungle. His jeans and shoes sloshed as he walked. The sounds of the jungle surrounded him: birds cawed, branches creaked and the wind rattled the palm fronds. There was a stream and he figured why not see. So, he knelt, cupped his hands and tasted it. "Mmm," fresh water. Then, he stripped and went in.

The stream was barely three feet deep, but it was fresh water. He splashed around and rinsed his hair out. Then, he filled his mouth and swished, "oh yeah." A crane zoomed by. "Nice," he splashed his hair and then shook the water out. "Should I tell her?" He smiled wide, "no."

Back at the beach, Claire looked around. She edged up and saw her luggage just up from the water's edge. So, she ripped the tear wider and put the gauze on her cut. It wasn't too bad a cut; maybe three inches long and a clean slice. Her hands trembled and she tucked the gauze into her capris. Then, she pulled the end around and did it again. "Ha," she knotted it and then tried to stand. Her ankles were pale. "Get your legs up he said." She sneered. "Not getting any air … moron." She limped to her bag and pulled it up the beach. She got it upright, pulled the handle out and tried to wheel it through the sand.

The bag's wheels dug in and she tried to lift it up. Then, she tried to wheel it again. "In Bermuda, you just yell and people come to do this." She lifted the best she could, but that wasn't enough to get it to roll. So, she dragged it and limped a foot or so at a time. "Damn that man." She got the bag settled, changed into shorts and looked around for … "Where is that man?"

Bill rested on the sand. "Nice," he sighed.

"There you are." Her eyes widened.

He leapt up and covered himself with his hands.

"Oh my God!" She turned away. "I was so right about you!"

"Taking a bath, fresh water here." He got a handful and tossed it at her.

"Sex addict, the minute you get some time alone, you strip!" She scoffed and limped away, "You terrible man!"

"Go away!" He shook off the anxiety attack, got his things and got dressed. His feet begged not to be put in soggy shoes and they were so wrinkled and pale that he gave in. "Alright, for now."

An hour or so had passed when he walked up to her. "I think were on an atoll or island."

Her luggage was open and some of her clothes lay on her luggage to dry out.

"Though it was waterproof." He laughed.

"Water resistant and they're just damp." She shook her head. "Look, didn't you say there was a radio or something in there?" She turned to him and then turned away. "Just signal them so we can get off this damned island."

"Sure lady." He grinned.

"Stop calling me that!" She turned on her side. "My leg's injured."

"You walked to the stream." He chuckled, went to the trunk and got the radio.
She sighed, "I was desperate …"

"Wondered about that." He smiled slyly.
"Oh, you are gross." She flipped him off. "Just get the radio and get us help."

"Yes, master." He bowed. "I ain't want ah beatin."

Her eyes burned right through his skin. "Can't you just be helpful?" She squinted, "You *little* people … you get some power, some authority and it all goes to your head."

"Fine, I'll get you some water, try the radio, build you a hut and round up some vittles." He marched off to the stream with the radio and an empty water pack. "Be real good, I ain't want ah whippin!" He disappeared into the jungle.

Chapter 5: Buried Treasure

Bill stumbled over a dead limb and then stepped on sticker grass. "Ah!" He jumped. "Damn, sticker grass." His feet had seen better days after soaking in ocean water. He sat down and looked his poor foot over; several stickers were embedded it. "Why didn't you stick her when she came through here?" He plucked, pulled, and then flicked them off. "Dumb things."

Claire drug her luggage a little further up the beach. She wanted it by the tree line. Waves rolled over the yellow blob of a raft and made it sad to be stuck there. She looked back and wondered about how to get it further up on the beach. Then, she turned and her leg gave out, "damn it!" She rested on the sand and rubbed her injury. "Why the hell am I stuck her with that idiot!"

Bill rubbed his foot, got up and made his way to the stream. "Martin was more fun." He filled the water pack. "What a horrible human being she is." He looked around and stared at something, something that wasn't part of the island. "What's that?" He set the water pack down and crossed the stream. "What the?" He looked at a tree about mid-way up, ten feet from the ground. His eyes focused on a mark on the trunk. It was a black mark etched into the coconut tree's light skin.

He walked back and squinted, then rubbed his eyes to get them to focus. "Alright, tree's not too tall." He studied the trunk. Then he got his hands around it, got his feet on the natural wedges that protruded from the trunk and went up. Slowly, he edged higher and higher. Something snapped, a branch or something. He jumped and then looked behind him. "Maniac woman," he muttered and then went up few more inches. The mark was just above his head. His eyes panned the trunk in front of him and then he leaned back as much as he could. His weight pulled the coconut tree and it swayed. His arms locked on and he pulled himself back to the trunk so that his chest was firmly implanted on the tree, "whoa!"

Claire looked around and wondered where Bill might be though she felt better to have the time to herself. She turned this way and that way to make sure he wasn't around. Then, she reached into her luggage and got a portrait out of a teenage boy, perhaps fourteen or fifteen. She kissed the boy's forehead and hugged the picture, "May see each other soon." She wiped the tears from her eyes, "I had a nice time in France." She moved her fingers across his soft face and then stroked his dark hair. "Champs Elysees was my favorite place, Cartier and Louis Vuitton … oh and my luggage *is* water proof." She looked around to be sure Bill hadn't snuck up on her. "I remembered that shirt you liked so much at Ichael Studio, so I …" She choked on her tears and got the shirt from her luggage. The smell made her smile and the feel reminded her of him. "I know you don't like me to buy you things when you're not there, but I just saw it and …" She looked around again. "I remember you had your eye on it." She folded it neatly, tucked it back in her bag and wiped her eyes. "Where the hell is that mad man?" She got to her feet, but her leg gave out, "Owe!"

Bill looked at the symbol and his eyes were fixed like a cat ready to pounce on a chick freshly pushed out of the nest. "AH!" His foot slipped and down he went. His lungs got the wind knocked out of them, but a big gulp of air whooshed in. "Damn it!" The symbol was fresh in his head. "No way," he rubbed the cut on his forehead that formed a dark red hue through the wrap that Martin tied round his head. Then, he sniffed his hand. He reached up and touched the cut again, brought his fingers to his nose, "man, that's not a good smell." His face, sunburned and peeling, was hot, feverish. He looked around to mark the spot; the jungle looked like jungle all around him, heavy trees and brush. For a second, he lost his bearings and then he heard the trickle of water.

"Claire!" he stumbled towards the beach. "Claire!"

The sun shined and her stomach growled. She ate one of the three remaining snack bars. "Person!" The yellow blob was half on the beach and half in the water. She looked at the blob and wondered whether to pull it up more, but it was so heavy. "Person! What was his name?" She turned and felt her leg, "ouch." There was a faint red color where blood soaked through the bandage and into her shorts. "My gosh, another pair ruined."

"Claire!" Bill stumbled.

"What the hell is he yelling for?" She edged up on her side again. "Yes, maniac!"

Bill didn't hear her and rubbed his head. The fever had him. He stumbled onto the beach.

"You drunk?" She managed to stand. "My leg hurts and there's more blood."

He looked her over and then fell.

"What's the matter with you?" She looked him over.

"Fever," he said. He looked at the sky and it spun slowly. "From my cut, it's … infected."

She swallowed a big gulp of fear and turned to the ocean. "Let's get that radio on and …" She held her hand up to block the sun. "They're out there."

"Who?" He flailed and gasped to catch his breath. Sweat rained down his forehead past his cheeks.

"Rescuers," she kept her eyes on the water that went to the horizon. "They're coming and …" She looked at him. "They'll help you." Her hands trembled. "I mean, I don't know first aid."

"Okay, just help me back to the tree line." He sat up. "I need some water."

"Sure, okay." She got a water pack and set it in his hand. "There you go."

"That salve, it's in the first aid bag." He tried to focus.

She looked and limped off. "Sure!" She got it and brought it to him.

"Just help me to the tree line and …" He shook his head. "Bring the first aid pack."

She looked at the pack, "it's too heavy."

"Just the first aid stuff, not the whole trunk." He fought to get to his feet. "Some serious bacteria are eating my brain."

"Ah!" She let out. "Just," her hands slammed together and wrenched one over the other frantically. "I … you need a doctor." Her sunburned wrinkles crunched together when she looked at him. Her anxiety climbed, "where's the radio?" She went through the trunk. "Where's that damn radio!"

"It's in there." He got on all fours and then stood. "It's … the first aid."

"Can't you just get it?" She looked up the beachhead at him. He fought to keep his balance. "Why don't you just come here and get it?" He teetered.

"Just come and get the God damned thing!" She turned and looked through the pack. There, it was there right under her hand. She snatched it up. "Oh, okay I've got it."

"First aid," he muttered and his face was dark with darker circles under his eyes. A drop of blood edged down the side of his face from the cut. He scratched the cut, "owe." He looked at the tree line, a blurry green mess, "please."

She froze, "stop saying that!"

"What?"

"Please … don't plead from me." She bit at her lower lip and then brought the first aid kit to him.

"Huh?" He took a step towards the trees.

"Go, just go!" She ordered and walked past him.

"You're a lot of help." He shook his head.

She limped towards the tree line with determination and muttered the words, "I'm no help."

The wind pushed against his back and he walked step over step slowly towards the tree line which was some distance from the water. "Maybe, when you get me …"

"You do it yourself; you get there." She belched out the words. "I'm just bringing the … this stuff." She was at the tree line and tossed the kit against a large coconut tree.

"Wow, okay." He had some of his senses, but the fever made him dizzy. "Where's the raft?"

She turned and looked. "It's like on the beach and, I don't know."

"Can't lose it." He got to the tree and plopped down. His fingers worked to get the salve open. "Help me put this on."

She looked at him and her face paled. "No." Her hands wrenched over one another.

"What?" He fought to shake off the fever and gently shook his head.

Her hands were lost within each other. "I mean, you're the …" She lost the words.

"What?" His fingers worked on the cap and, finally, got it off. "Need the aspirin."

"See, you know better than me." She stepped back.

"Need a new bandage," he pulled at the one wrapped around his head. It came off and a putrid smell made his nose ache. The cut was a couple inches long, very red and swollen. He poured some water over it and a trickle of saturated blood and junk dripped down the side of his face. "That sucks."

She got the remaining gauze from the first aid kit and realized that she'd used most of it. "Oh," she looked at what was left. "Here, here it is." She tossed it to hm. "I'm just not good at helping people."

The fever was a hardened storm that pushed past his head down through his face. "Couldn't hand it to me?" He shook his head once and then got the gauze. "Need more than that."

"Yes, okay." She got her dirty capris, ripped them and gave him a stretch of cloth.

He looked at it and his mouth hung open, "thanks."

She nodded and stayed a few feet away. "You, you just know what to do, so do it." Her hands were locked together and her knuckles paled. "Oh, the radio." She got it and looked it over. "Just tell me how to turn it on."

His eyes widened as much as they could. He couldn't believe her. "I … don't know."

A strong gale blew sand all over them.

"The wind." She covered her eyes. "Damn sand. Be glad if I never see sand again."

"Another storm," he looked at the clouds that gathered some miles away; they were dark and surely had a lot of rain tucked in them. "Great." He wiped the heavy sweat from his brow and tried to focus. "Get this salve on my …" His words drifted away and his face boiled.

"I have an umbrella." She limped off to her luggage, got an umbrella out and her poncho.

Bill shook his head at her. "What … what's she …" The fever made his head throb. Then, he fell back on the sand. The sky spun around and he squeezed the tube. A blob of salve squirted onto his fingers; he smeared it all over the cut and the side of his head.

"Here, I've … you can have it." She put the poncho over him.

"Any aspirin?"

"I … I don't know." She fumbled through the first aid kit. "Oh, yes … here you go."

The infection seeped into his head and played horrid games with his imagination.

"Ah!" He shouted. "You see!"

She jumped! "What?" The sickness was too much for her and she went to her luggage, got hold of the handle and was determined to drag it and her away from him.

"Treasure!" He shouted and then laughed. "Ah!"

She looked at him and the poncho flew up. "No," she turned and the storm was nearly there. Bits of rain tapped the sand around them. She moved as fast as she could to get the poncho and help him. The poncho was just a few feet from him; she grabbed it, put it over him and tucked it around his chest and legs. "Just keep this on you." She pulled at it. "Gosh, you can do it. You don't need my help, you just don't need it … you don't *want* my help."

She rushed back to her bag, got it in the tree line and got another poncho out.

"Treasure!" Bill shouted. "Treasure!"

She looked at him and pursed her lips. "You're fine!" Her hands held each other tightly. "I can't." She mumbled, "I can't do it again." She covered her ears. "I won't."

He turned and flailed his hands as he talked. "My head … my head is on fire!"

She looked at him and wiped her tears away. "You don't want my help." Her body trembled from fear and not the cool air that came with the thunderstorm. The rain drops streamed down her face and cooled her burned skin along with nightfall.

"Treasure!" He shouted and then his shouts turned into ramblings. "Symbol, I saw it."

The downpour and the wind thrashed her umbrella! "What?" She looked at him and his hands shot up and then fell to his sides.

"It was there, a symbol." He said and looked into nothingness. His face was a puddle of rain water and his eyes were bloodshot. "On the tree, there it was … treasure."

"I … my help never worked out." She found a small bottle of aspirin her luggage. "Just this once, I'll help you." She went to him, knelt and turned the bottle over; white clumps of aspirin slid out. "Oh no, they … it's all mush." Her hands trembled and she put the bottle to his mouth. "Just swallow, please." She gasped. "Just …"

"Don't plead with me." Their eyes locked.

"Oh God," she dropped the bottle and it rolled off of him as easily as the drops rolled off of the poncho. "I can't. I'm sorry, so sorry, but I can't." Her good leg lifted her and her sore one helped. She stood and looked him over. She knelt, pulled the poncho over his arms and tucked it deep under him. She took her umbrella and jammed the end into the sand so that it covered his face. "I'm sorry." She wiped the wet from her face. "But, I don't want … I can't help you anymore." She turned, didn't need any help from the wind to walk off and left him. "I'm no good helping people!"

"On the tree, high up." He mumbled. "On the tree, they scratched it!"

"On the tree," she went to her luggage, emptied it onto the ground and sat one end up. She got her son's picture and wiped it off. Then, she got under the luggage. "Not this time, God." She looked at the thunder clouds. "Not again!" She shouted at the clouds.

"On the tree!" He shouted and then mumbled gibberish. "Tree scratched, they scratched the tree."

Lightning and thunder echoed over them and around them. Rain shot this way and that way with the wind as it ran reckless up the beach and across the island. The night crawled along and the storm pummeled them.

She kept her head down and looked at the picture. She wiped the wet from her face despite the rain that blew in and made her face all wet again. Drops slid down the glass past her son's face. "I can't save him; you know it."

"Scratched the tree!" Bill yelled. The infection chewed on him and he spat out wild words. He wiggled his hands inside the poncho and lifted his head in a rage. "Ah!"

She jumped and hugged the picture. "I can't."

"On the tree!" He screamed.

"Shut up!" She yelled over the thunder and over the wind that howled through the jungle!

Bill caught his breath and lowered his head. Then, he calmly said, "help me."

She brought her knees up and tucked the picture between her knees and bosom. Then, she covered her ears and closed her eyes.

The wind wailed and lashed the island, lashed at Claire and lashed at Bill!

"Help me." His hands pushed hard to get free and his brain cried out. "Help me!" He yelled. The virus bit him and with every bite, he jerked and kicked and cried out, "AH!"

"SHUT UP!" She yelled, "JUST SHUT UP!" She bobbed her head up and down. "Shut up, please just shut up." She held the picture tight against her bosom. "I'm not helping you!" She looked at the boy's face, "tell him … I'm no good at helping people."

Her son's eyes and hers met.

"I can't." She wiped the rain from her face.

The boy in the picture looked at her and his baby browns were soft and full.

She swallowed hard.

"Scratched me!" Bill yelled.

Her eyelids slammed shut, "God." She opened her eyes, looked at her son and nodded, "okay, I'll try."

The storm thrashed the island, but the thunder was past and the lightning jolts were softer.

She got up, got herself right and limped over to Bill.

"Help me," he kicked and shivered.

"I'm here." She looked him over. "I'm here."

"I'm here." He repeated. His legs kicked and his arms jerked under the poncho.

"So," she sat down. "What scratched the tree?"

"Scratched!" He yelled and his legs jerked and kicked!

She jumped, got a piece of her torn up capris and put some water on it. "Okay," she dabbed his forehead. "What got scratched?"

His eyes danced around. "The tree."

"So, what about it." She looked Bill over and licked sadness from her lips. "What happened with the tree?"

"They, they marked it." He said and closed his eyes.

"You're a strong person." She looked up and closed her eyes. Then, she opened them and looked at

him. "Bill."

"Bill," he said.

"So, why did they scratch the tree?" She fidgeted with the cloth.

"So, they'd know, they'd know the way." He let out and then turned over.

"Okay," she kept her hands to herself. "It's okay."

He licked his wet lips. "Going to die."

She looked at him. "No," she looked back at her luggage. "No, they're coming."

"Going to get their treasure." He said.

"I …" She hesitated. "I had treasure once."

"You know it then?" He wrestled with the poncho.

"I had a son." She pursed her lips and fought the feelings that told her it was personal, too personal for just anyone.

"Had a son?"

The rain drops were more mist like and thick clouds hung over them.

She wiped her eyes. "Mark."

"Treasure," Bill said.

"Yes, he was. He was my treasure and then … he was gone." She looked away. "We … my husband didn't want to go." She licked her lips. "He never wanted to do anything with his son."

Bill mumbled, "Treasure."

She laid the wet cloth on his forehead and patted his arm. "He worked." She gritted her teeth. "Even when he came home and I said spend time with your son." Her hands tightened. "He was more interested in work … or *things* at work."

"Treasure," he mumbled and the word faded.

"He was a treasure." She caught her breath and her feelings. "So, I took him. I … we went to South America, because he … we liked to travel."

Bill huffed.

"His dad wouldn't do those dad and son things, so I took him." She looked at the jungle and into the darkness. There, her memory came to life. She and Mark were zip lining. Then, "We went snorkeling and swimming … fishing though I didn't care for it." She looked around them. "I didn't want him to miss out on the stuff boys do just because his father was an ass …" She cleared her throat. "He was."

Bill kicked at the poncho.

"So, we went hiking in the Amazon." She looked up. "And we got more and more adventurous with each trip."

The wind brushed up against her gently and the rain stopped.

"He, we were hiking and he fell." Her tears mixed with the rain on her face.

"Mark," Bill said.

"Yes, that's his name." She turned away. "Mark and I had this guide who …" She took a deep breath and then let it out slow. "I've never said a word about what happened."

Bill's hands fought under the poncho.

She saw his hand twist and turn under the poncho, so she lifted it and took his hand. "It's going to be okay … I think."

Waves crashed onto the beach.

"The guide …I asked, I mean I checked him out and he said he knew this great place." She made a fist. "He led us into the mountains and Mark fell." She hit her fist on the sand. "He fell." She broke down and there were more tears than the storm had rain. "He fell!"

"Mark," Bill said and his grip tightened around hers.

"His leg, he broke his leg and the guide went for help." She wiped the tears away. "He went for help, but didn't come back."

"Mark," Bill said.

"The break … it got infected and my son died." She gritted her teeth together. "When they found us, it was a couple days later."

Palm fronds rubbed against each other to comfort themselves now that the storm was over.

"So," she said. "You see, it's better that I don't help you." She pulled her hand from his. "Sleep, just sleep." She tucked his hand back under the poncho.

Bill's eyes were closed, but he was not asleep. The virus raged through him.

She got up, went to her luggage and got her picture. Then, she got a windbreaker on and went back to Bill. She leaned against a palm tree and held her son's picture against her bosom. "He died last year and … Paris was his favorite place." She kissed her son's cheek.

Chapter 6: I Hate that Man and Rum Cure's All

The night passed with Bill's body, mind and soul in a rage against the stench that took even bigger bites of him.

Claire put a cool cloth on his head. "Keep fighting." She pushed the picture into the sand to hold it upright and the moon reflected off Mark's face. "You'll stay with me, help me." She smiled at him.

"Ah!" Bill groaned in agony.

Claire jumped. "You're as loud as Mark was."

The late night passed into the early morning hours and then the gleam of orange rays burst over the horizon.

She looked at Bill who trembled off and on.

He mumbled occasionally and she looked at her son's picture. "You did that when you were hurt." She wiped her eyes. "Made me think you were going to be okay." Her fist tightened and she got up.

Bills slowly opened his eyes.

"That man …" She shook her fist and went into a sudden rage. "I hate that man!"

He turned his head just slightly and saw her in a fit.

"He left us!" She kicked at the sand with her good leg and nearly fell over. "DAMN THAT MAN!" She shook her fists, "AH!" A scream of all that pent-up emotion roared through her, "AH!"

Bill turned his head back and closed his eyes.

The sun's orange glow slid up her face and revealed her anger. "Ah!" She yelled and her throat ached. "I ..." She hesitated, turned and looked at Bill, then looked at the sun. "I hired someone to find that man, that horrible man who left us." She wiped her emotions from her nose and mouth. "I won't lie Mark. I wanted him to suffer, to die." She clenched her fist so tightly that she would have to spend hours getting her fingers to work again.

Bill opened his eyes once more and looked at the stars that slowly faded away.

"I'm sorry, but I wanted him to die!" She stormed around with a limp every time she set that foot down.

Bill turned his head towards her and his brow went up.

"I hope he *burns* in hell." She let out and looked back at Bill.

Bill quickly closed his eyes and froze.

She uttered the words again through her pursed lips. "I hope he *burns*." She fanned her face, went to her luggage and got a prescription out. She downed a couple pills and a drink of water.

The sun lit the island up and then forced the clouds to give way. The brilliant blue sky made the white beach and gently rolling waves into a paradise. The gentle breezes eased around Claire who passed out next to her Gucci luggage after her emotional rant and with the help of a sleep aid.

He cleared his throat quietly and tried to move, but couldn't. He edged his hands up and then realized that he was held down by the poncho. His heart jumped and he fought to get free. The poncho headpiece flapped with the wind and covered his face! He yelled, "Ah!" Then, he kicked and thrashed about until he got the sides pulled out from under him. "I ain't burning in hell you rotten filth." The poncho gave out and he jerked to his side, sat up and tore it from him! "I'm free!"

Claire was sound asleep.

"AH!" He roared.

She didn't move.

Birds in the jungle cawed and cried out.

"Want me to die, you hateful - filthy woman." He seethed at the thought that he saved her, helped her and then she thought he should die. He looked her over and saw that she was still out. "Alright then," he got his wits about him and hurried to the first aid kit, got a Swiss Army Knife and the last pack of water. He drank all of it. "Let her figure it out, cockroach." He went to the trunk. "There's gonna be a line, honey." He waved his hand at her and dragged his heel in the sand. "You better not cross it!" He looked the beach over. "Great, she let the raft go." His face boiled. "You ain't going to get me honey, no you're not." He got a tarp, rope, a couple snack bars, an orange plastic grab bag and the radio. "Set a trap for Mrs. Cockroach and see if I die." That was it. He turned and marched into the jungle.

Claire drew in a deep breath and her nose wrinkled as she snored.

Bill stomped through the jungle, "ah!" He jerked his barefoot up. "Damn it." A sand sticker got him. He flicked it out. "Why don't you stick her?" He looked around and saw a few of the sticker grasses. "Dumb plant," he hopped over one and then another until he was past them. "Damn, my shoes." He looked back and shook his head. "Who needs them?" He walked off.

That afternoon, Claire turned, stretched and then sat up. Dried tears were a sandy white trail down her cheeks; she rubbed them from her eyes. "Hello?" The poncho blew up towards the tree line. She fought to get to her feet and couldn't. "Alright, just like in Tai-Chi, hands out front … sway, then up!" She kicked and got to her feet. "Ah," her injured leg trembled, but she stiffened it up. "Hello!"

Bill stopped at the stream and filled his water. Then, he stripped to his boxers, slid into the cool fresh water and sunk his head under. His fingers scrubbed the junk from his hair and then rubbed the raw sunburn on his face. Bubbles yelled and burst from his mouth as he let his anger out. Then, he came up and was clean. "Ah!" The bandage floated away from him.

Claire turned towards the jungle and looked. "Hello," she bit at her lip. "God, what *was* his name?"

The coconut trees and ground palms were pretty to look at, but deeper in the jungle; things were shady, dark and mysterious.

She looked around to get an idea of where she was and then headed into the jungle. "Jim?" She looked up. "Rob?" She rubbed her face, "I can't think this early. I need water." She looked for the first aid pack and then a puzzled look grabbed her. "Where?" Her eyes panned the beach and then she saw the trunk. "Oh, there it is." Her legs carried her swiftly to the trunk and then she stopped suddenly. "Storm must've moved it.". She pondered, "oh God." Then, she frantically looked up and down the beach. "The floaty thing!" She looked all over, "Where's the yellow blob?"

Bill spat water out of his mouth. "Wish I could drink it all and let her figure it out." Then, there was a hard thump behind him. "Hey!" He turned and the jungle was quiet.

Then, the birds cawed and cried out. "THUMP!"

Bill jerked the other way and … nothing. "What the heck?"

Wherever the thump happened, the birds stopped their happy caws.

He looked all around the jungle. "Claire, I know what you're up to." He crept out of the stream on the other side. "THUMP!" He jumped, "You won't get me!"

Claire looked at the jungle. "Hey, you!" She opened the trunk and there wasn't any water. "Water, where's the water?" She went to where Bill lay for the night and looked at his footprints. "Where did he go?"

"THUMP!" Bill saw it this time. "Oh, damn." A laugh burst out of him riding on the back of fear. "Coconuts, dur." He got up the stream, went to the coconut and picked it up. "Damn, they're big."

"THUMP!"

He ducked! "Dangerous damn things too!" Then, a sinister thought overtook him. "Bet I could knock her out with one." A smile slyly crossed is reddish brown face and then he took a drink. Water dripped from his mouth and he felt his chin whiskers. "You see movies about life on a deserted island." Then, he sniffed himself and his nose turned up. "I don't think anyone really appreciates just how foul people are when they don't shower or shave for days." His hair was a ragged mop; wet, sand ridden, and oily. He touched his hair. "No," his fingers trebled. "Coconut milk?" Then, his stomach let out a growl! "Whoa," he rubbed his tummy. "That's the other part of being on an island. What the hell do you eat?" He looked at the coconut trees. "Get hit on my head and I'm done for … unless my hair is so oily that the coconut skids off." He got dressed.

"Person!" Claire stood at the edge of the jungle. She covered her mouth and looked at the shadows. Some strange bird cawed and she jumped! "Ah!" She pointed her finger at the bird. "When I was in South American, you tasted exactly like chicken with hot sauce, okay." Her body froze and her eyes panned the dense jungle.

The wind rustled the palm fronds and they rattled one after the other.

"I can't. I just can't." She stepped back. "Helpful person!" The wind pushed her towards the jungle and she backed away. "Jungle got my son, maybe not this jungle, but one that had trees, strange sounds, and darkness at its core." She bit at her lip. "Son, I can't go in there … it's too much like where we went." She stepped back and fell over the poncho that Bill threw off of him. "Ah!" Fear gripped her by her arms and pulled her back. "Man person!" She yelled. "What the hell is his name!"

Bill looked back and it wasn't his name he heard; it was some creature that cracked branches. "What the hell is that?" His arm drew back and had the coconut ready to smash whatever it was. "No one likes a chicken." He stepped back and another branch broke somewhere around him. He muttered the words, "bawk, bawk, bawk."

"THUMP!" A coconut slammed the ground behind him.

"Damn it!" He jerked around. His reddish-brown skin paled. "Judas Priest."

Claire found a couple of snack bars in the trunk and ate them up. The water pack near her luggage had some water, but not enough to save her. She drank it. "Man person!"

Darkness crept up the ocean waves right to the beach where it sat quietly. Claire wiped her eyes. "I … what do I do?" She went through her luggage, took nearly everything out and then was surprised. "Oh!" A bottle of water was in hand. "Oh, I'm so glad I didn't throw you out." It was full and she quickly got the cap off. "A gin and tonic would be better, but I am so glad to have water." Her lips stung a little and she drank half the bottle before she tipped it back. "Better save some for later."

Bill was on the other side of the stream. The tarp lay halfway over the rope that he tied off between two tree trunks; then, he anchored the ends of the tarp with the coconuts. The tent was quite nice. His little stash had two snack bars, the radio and an orange bag with matches and a flashlight. "Sweet," he muttered and set the things aside.

"THUMP!"

His anxiety jumped, but he knew it was a coconut. "She ain't coming out here this time of night."

Darkness lost its patience with Claire and saw that she wasn't going into the jungle. So, it swarmed up the beach and over the island in an instant.

Claire's eyes reflected off the moonlight. She wiped the tears away. "Man person?" The breezes gently went past her and the ocean was a calm gray mass that went into infinity. "Mark, what do I do?"

The jungle barked and cawed often. Strange noises were louder at night and she put her luggage between her and the beasts in the jungle. "Mark," she said and some sadness overcame her. Her eyes looked up at the stars and it was there she swallowed her anger. "My son Mark, God." She looked at the sky. Her stomach turned. "He died … I, I blamed you." She looked down and wiped her eyes. "I miss him so much." The wind pushed her. "That guy is in there." She looked at the jungle and the jungle stared right back at her. "Mark died in a jungle and I just can't bring myself to go in there."

The waves slapped the beach and the palm fronds rustled with every gust of wind.

"You can tell me to all you want, but I'm not going in there; it's dark." She rubbed her eyes and then looked at the moon. "It's not even a full moon and why'd he go off and leave me anyways?" Fear surged through her. "I didn't leave him, well, I did, but I came back." She took a swig of water. "I stayed with him just like I stayed with my son."

The waves were bigger, heavier and crashed against the sand!

Claire jumped. "You took him." She wiped her mouth and nose. "You did."

Bill sat up and shook off the bits of sand, grass and wet that clung to him. "Go mess with someone else." He looked across the stream towards the beach.

The night sky was clear enough that the moon's craters looked deep and ominous.

He pursed his lips and sighed. "She said terrible stuff." He shook his head. "I mean to say oh, I wish he was dead." The wind rattled the tarp. "Yeah, right. She doesn't deserve my help."

Claire got a Dior blouse on and sniffed it. "Not the most pleasant smell for Dior." She reached in her luggage and got a bottle of perfume out. "I don't need to read it, I know the shape of this bottle, Annick Goutal, Eau d'Hadrien." The bottle was petite with beautiful ridges that shined against the moonlight. "Hundred and twenty dollars an ounce," she sighed. "Who's going to notice it here?" She sprayed once on her neck. "Better to smell beautiful than to smell ..." Her nose cringed and then she held the sprayer near her nose. "Oh, so lovely." She gently drew her hand across the nozzle and smelled it. A relaxed sigh slipped past her lips.

Bill turned on his side and then turned again to his other side. "I can't believe how bad I stink." He sat up, licked his forefinger and held it up and outside the tarp. "Have to sleep upwind from myself." The wind blew towards his head and so he turned himself around. "Alright wind, don't change direction." He took a couple of sniffs before he lay down, "okay."

By morning, the gentle breezes were heavier and some of Claire's clothes blew down the beach. She sat up and rubbed the sleep from her eyes. "Hey?" Then, her tummy growled and she touched it, "got to have something to eat ... snack bars." She got to her feet, got her sandals on and saw her things. "Hey, my clothes on the ... damn sand!" She hurried and got them picked up. Then, she tucked everything away in her luggage, checked herself the best she could and got the picture of Mark from her luggage. "I'm going to do it." Her determination showed up as strong lines across her forehead and her pursed lips. She put lip balm on and used up what moisturizer she had left. "You stay here, but I'm going." She set his picture back in her luggage. "Man person!" It was time. "How hard can his name be?" The water bottle sat at her feet. "Oh," she grabbed it and looked around to be sure she had everything. "Bob?"

Bill licked his dry lips and his skin peeled. He ran his hands over his face and felt the weird little rolled up things that were his dead skin. "Gross man, dead skin." He looked at his hands and his eyes widened. "I'm peeling?" He sat up, "the last time I peeled, I was in Ft. Lauderdale, summer of two thousand - seven." His hair was a dried out, a dark colored stringy mop thing. His fingers tried to do anything to get through his hair. "Wow, now what." He got up and dusted himself off. "Breakfast first." There were coconuts here and there. He grabbed one and tried to cut through the shell with the pocketknife. "NatGeo special … how to survive on a deserted island." His eyes wandered the jungle landscape. There was a large rock with some curved edges. He sat down right next to the rock, raised the coconut overhead and brought it down on the rock! The husk cracked. "Okay," up the coconut went and then, "CRACK!"

"Bob!" She looked back at the beach. "My God, I'm not stupid!" She turned and looked at the faded dark line that separated the beach from the jungle. "Don't scare me." She held her foot out and took a step. "Blaine!"

Bill peeled the husk off and then went to work on the other side. Before long, the coconut cracked open! Coconut milk splashed out and he drank every bit of it. "Wasn't so hard."

"Brian!"

He jerked to his side, "I'll be damned." He licked up the remaining milk that tried to cling to the inside of the coconut. "So, she's coming for me." He hurried to his makeshift tent, packed up and walked off.

"Buford!" She stood at the stream and tasted the water. "Is anyone really named Buford anymore?" The cool water drifted by. "Oh, thank goodness." She plunged the water bottle under until it was full. "Forgot that this was here." She looked for a way around the steam and then walked in. "Just water, no anacondas … I hope." She looked at the trees and the watery depth; it was waist deep. "Bradley!" The water slowly drifted by. "Isn't there a way around or a bridge?"

Bill looked back, tripped and fell into a pit that was a couple feet deeper than the ground around him. "Damn her, she's calling for Bradley … really?" He pushed up and the ground cracked like wood bent to its breaking point. "Sand doesn't crack like that." The sand slowly seeped into cracks in the ground. "What the?"

The ground gave out in loud cracks! Wood splinters and boards snapped! Bill fell into a pit. He hit one side of the pit, bounced and then slid down a few feet where several crates sat. "Are you serious!" The crates were marked with a heart that had something that looked like a number four at the top. "Any minute now, Johnny Depp will come out and ask about the rum." He looked himself over and seemed to be okay. Then, he laughed, dusted himself off and wiped the sand and junk from the top of one crate. "So, is it rum?"

Claire lifted her blouse, "not the Dior." She waded into the stream and her determination kept her going. She wiped the sweat from her face. "My gosh, the humidity."

Bill saw a piece of timber that fell in with him. He picked it up and hit the crate! The slats cracked and he pulled them apart. "No way," there were

bottles in it. He pulled one out and there was no label. The Swiss Army knife had a bottle opener tucked into it; he got it out, pushed the pointed end through the wax and dug into the cork. "Probably, couple hundred years old." He got a good grip and pulled. "POP," the cork came out and with it, an aroma of the most hardcore rum. "Oh man, this is crazy."

"Byron!" she had her hands cupped around her mouth. "Where do his people go on a deserted island?"

He sniffed the bottle. "Damn, burned the hair in my nose, whew." His lips locked around the end and he took a swig. A single swallow was all that got past his lips before he choked, "damn, no wonder every … one, was …" He fought to get his breath, which was soaked with alcohol. "Drunk," he licked the rum from his lips, "damn good."

"BILL!" The birds jumped at the noise she made. "Bill, that's his name." She smiled. "Bill!"

He looked up and squinted. "Good Lord, the bride of Frankenstein comes." He looked around the top. "Got to get out on my own." Then, he looked at the crates, "stack them?"

She walked past where he tented for the night and a sticker bush caught her foot. "Owe!"

Bill looked up the sides, "c'mon." The crates wobbled on top of each other.

She got the sticker out and went on. "Bill!"

Now, he heard her clearly. "Remembered my name finally." He got his foot on the edge of the crate and stepped up while he used his hands to climb. He pushed up, the crate gave way and he fell back into the pit. "Damn it!" The pain made him arch his back and convulse. "Man, nothing worse than a back scrape."

"Bill?" She heard something. "Bill?" She looked at the jungle and it all looked the same wherever she looked, shadows and trees and bush. "BILL!" She screamed this time and the birds covered their ears.

Bill was frustrated. His face scrunched up and his hands were tightly wound into fists. "Want me to die, cockroach."

She stumbled over a dead palm tree trunk. "Where is he?"

He got the stick he used to break the crate and looked up. "Help!"

"Bill?" She looked around and stopped. "BILL!"

"Down here," he said and wondered what she'd do. "Probably try to bury me alive, but I got the rum, honey."

"Bill, where are you?" She headed towards where she heard him.

"Here!" He held the stick up to bat her back to the beach. "HERE!"

She came over a small dune and saw the pit. "Oh my!" She scooted carefully up to the edge. "Bill?"

"Yeah," he moved to the side.

"Are you okay?"

"Not dead, if that's what you mean." He sneered at her.

"What else would I mean?" She leaned over and saw the stick. "What are you going to do with that stick."

"Well, you mentioned wanting me to die." He gritted his teeth. "Figured, I better be ready for you."

"What are you talking about?" The puzzled look on her face made Bill wonder.

"You said you wished I was dead." Anger warmed his face. "You said it when I was sick."

"I didn't say that." Her brow went up. "That's a terrible thing to say."

"It is." He eyed her.

Then, she gasped.

Bill locked eyes with her. "Uh-huh, you did say it."

She gulped, "well, yes."

"I knew it!" He shouted. "I saved you and fight off a shark and …"

"Hold on!" She stomped her foot and nearly fell in with him. "Just hold on a minute, I wasn't talking about you. I swear." Her face cooled.

"Right, because there's someone else on the island." He shook the stick at her.

"Is there?"

"No!" He swung the stick at her. "Stop being so literal."

"Truth be told, I … I was talking about a guide … see my son …" She licked her dry lips.

"Mark," he blurted out. "Mark is your son?"

She caught her breath. "Yes, Mark is my son."

"So, who did you want to die?" Bill slowly lowered the stick and then it all hit him.

She swallowed her upset. "I admit that it was a bad thing to say, but he left us." She sat down. "He left us!"

"Who left you?" Bill leaned against the wall to see her. "Who left you!"

"My husband didn't have time for our son. So, I took him on this hiking thing in South America. We, he saw it on some show he liked. So, I took him."

"Right, but that doesn't tell me who left him or about your rant the other night." Bill eyed her.

"We had a guide and my son fell." She fought the sadness and hurt. "He … his leg broke and the guide, he was supposed to go for help."

Bill set the stick down.

"Two days went by and … my son died. That afternoon a couple rescuers showed up." She wiped her eyes. "I wanted him to die, the guide … I wanted the guide to die, because he left me and my son."

"I'm sorry." Bill gently sighed.

"Mark … he told me to go for help, but I wouldn't leave him, I mean I couldn't leave him there." She pressed her hands against her face. "So, you see I wanted that guide to die, to burn in hell for leaving us, for leaving my son to die." She tried to smile. "I didn't want to care for you …"

"Because you were afraid it might happen again, but …"

"You're not my son." She finished.

Bill swallowed hard and ran his teeth along his lips. "I see now." He looked at the rum. "I am sorry."

"It's not your fault." She looked around the pit.

He cleared his throat, "sorry I left you on the beach. It's just, I felt like things were …"

"What? That I wanted you to die?" She shook her head. "No, I don't."

"It was foolish of me to think that." He held a bottle up. "I've got rum. Maybe, we should have a drink."

She leaned over the edge.

"Don't fall in!" His eyes widened.

"What do you want me to do?" She smiled.

He looked around. "My rope should be up there."

She pushed back and got up. A quick look around and there it was. "Okay," she picked it up.

"I think it's long enough. So, just tie it around a tree." He looked around to see where she went.

"Like I know how to make a knot." She got the rope up.

"You went on that hike; they must've made a knot there." He looked at the top edge of the pit.

"They did." She wrapped the rope around a coconut tree, tied it off and went to the pit. "Here!" She threw the rope over.

He got it, went to climb up and then looked at the rum. "Rum first!"

"What?"

The last crate was up and on top. Bill climbed up and out. The two of them stared at each other for a moment and then she held her arms out.

"Why not?" They hugged. "Thanks," he smiled.

She smiled and then stepped back. "Okay," it was better now, easier for her and him.

"Here," he got the pocketknife out, popped a cork and gave her a bottle.

"Can't remember the last time that I had a buzz." Claire looked at the end of the bottle, pulled her blouse up and used it to wipe off the lip of the bottle. "Probably after the divorce."

"We survived a plane crash." He smiled at the craziness of it all.

"We did." She smelled the rum, "alright." The end of the bottle went up, she swallowed and choked it all up.

Bill took a drink.

They coughed and choked!

"Jesus," Bill licked the remaining rum from his lips, "got some serious flavor."

"That what you call it." She coughed again. "You're growing a beard by the way."

"Yeah, well no razor on a deserted island." Bill took another swig and looked at her calves. "Seems, your legs aren't as smooth either." He smirked. "Now, we have to decide whether we want to signal for help or wait till we finish the rum off."

Her brow went up the same time that the bottle went to Bill's mouth.

Chapter 7: Rum and Reconciliation

They were drunk. She laughed wildly and Bill roared at the jungle!

"AH!" He blurted out, "pirates!"

"Where!" Claire grimaced, turned and feigned fear! "I hate the jungle!"

"Why, what's wrong with the jungle?" He coughed and rum came out of his nose!

There was a moment of quiet, they looked at each other and then their laughter roared again.

"That's so gross!" She belched!

"Oh, no you didn't!" Bill let out and then fell back against a fallen coconut tree. "So, how rich are you, lady?"

"I have money." She laughed, "I never said I was a lady." She floundered and fell backwards.

"Claire!" Bill tried to get up and tripped over his own feet. "Damn!"

"No lady would have married the dirt bag I found!" She slapped her leg, got herself back up and then took another drink. The rum trickled past her lips and down the sides of her face. "He … he blamed me for what …" The ends of her mouth turned down and she looked sad. "Hell with him!"

"Yeah, to hell with him!" Bill blurted. "Honey, he's a dirt bag."

"He is." She said and her words mushed together. "He … this slut that he … she worked for us."

"Oh no he didn't!" Bill took another swig and the bottle was half-full. "Honey, forget him."

"I want to. I ..." The words were there, but she stopped them and her cheeks blew up like a chipmunk with all those words rear-ending each other at the back of her throat.

"What?" Bill squinted. "Your cheeks are huge!"

She huffed, "He blamed me and took that admin whore for a wife."

"Blamed you?" Bill couldn't focus. "For what?"

She looked at him and then her face was plain, lost in thought. "For everything."

"He's a damned cockroach." Bill said and held his bottle up. "Cheers to that!"

"One of those cockroaches that ..." She caught her breath and then her sun burn paled. "He's ..."

Bill's eyes widened.

"He's ..." She sucked in her cheeks and convulsed!

"Vomit?" Bill asked.

Claire vomited. "Ah!" She spat.

"Oh honey," he went to her and put his arm around her.

She turned to him and a bit of vomit fell from her lips and onto his arm.

"Gross." He felt the horror in his own stomach just looking at her. "Water, you need some water."

"I need," she dry heaved, drew her arm across her mouth and wiped the leftover onto her blouse.

"Oh, that *was* pretty." Bill stumbled to the water and got it.

Claire looked his butt over, smiled and then passed out.

"Here," he turned and she was out cold. "Oh damn," he said, crawled to her and then his nose turned; the smell of puke. "Okay, she had to let it out and now she has to sleep it ..." His stomach kicked and then he vomited all over her stomach and boobs! "Blah!" He looked the mess over and then looked at the water bottle. "Here ... here's some water." He poured the water on his vomit and it just moved the vomit around on her. "Shi ..." he muttered and looked around. The island turned sideways and then he passed out.

Some native birds gathered; they cawed and screamed at the sight of two humans who had vomited and peed themselves on their island. No number of screams or caws would wake Claire or Bill from their drunken stupor. The sun set, the night came and the birds rested along with Claire and Bill.

Morning, Claire turned. Sand was in her hair and on her cheek. Stomach junk had dried and rolled off her to the ground where it joined the vomit chorus. Bill's vomit had soaked in her Dior blouse. She licked her lips and then chewed on grains of sand. Her tongue tried to push the junk out, but didn't get it. She sat up. A hangover kicked in and thrust her head into a brick wall, "ah." She moaned and gently massaged her temples.

Bill was out and sucked in gulps of air, then, like a bellows, he blew them out.

She looked him over and then looked around. Was it the same day or had they slept through the night?

The sun shined brightly over them and the birds were kinder when they cawed and cried.

"Tech person," she said gently. "You."

He turned and his arms flopped over one another. Half his face rested against the sand and the other half faced the sun.

"Bill," she tried to sit up and then the hangover punched her. "Owe, owe, owe," she pressed her fingers to her forehead. "Water."

Bill coughed, "wants me to die, buh, buh, buh."

She looked at him and shook her head gently. "Where's the water?"

Bill yawned and fought to sit up. "Hey," he looked her over and then his eyes widened when he saw the dried vomit all over her blouse.

"Need some water." She said and crawled to the bottle.

"Yeah, right there." He tried to lift his hand to point and didn't have the strength. "Talk about a drunken stupor."

"It's always the same." She said, got the water and guzzled. "You have a great time drinking and laughing, but when you wake up the next day, you regret it."

Bill nodded.

She looked herself over, "oh my God?"

"Yeah," he said. "You threw up."

"On myself!" She pulled at clean spot on her blouse, "This *was* Dior couture." Her hand came close, but didn't touch the dried stains. "Now, it's Dior vomit."

"Nice pattern," Bill gulped and rubbed forehead. "Monster hangover."

She looked herself over again and then shook her head. "Owe," she touched her head gently. "I'll be upset later; I've got to change."

"Have some water and then we'll head back to the beach." He got to his knees and then got up. "I think there's more than rum buried here."

She looked up at him. "Oh, like what?"

He grinned slyly and his eye brows shot up and down.

"You can't be serious." She looked around and then looked into the pit.

"I think that after we get cleaned up, we should come back and have a look around." He smiled.

"Uh, that's well and good, but we need food." She drank the water. "We need to be rescued."

"Yeah, you're right." His mouth was nasty and he looked at the water. "You mind?"

"No, did you throw up too?" She asked. "Leaves a gross taste in your mouth."

"Yeah, but I … my junk is over there." He glanced in the jungle.

She looked at her blouse and then looked at him. "Rum was good, but Dior is better."

"So, you okay to walk back?" He looked her over. "You've got sand stickers in your hair."

She reached up to get them out.

Bill yelped. "No! You'll get pricked."

"Oh, alright." She walked back to him.

"I'll get them." He handed her the water and picked each one out. His nose jerked when he got a whiff of his vomit on her blouse and he dry heaved.

"Sorry," she said and fanned her bosom.

"Oh, it's … don't worry about it." He forced himself to smile.

By mid-morning, they moved their things closer to the jungle. Then, they went to the stream and washed off. She changed into another blouse that she called, "street wear" and Bill walked around in his boxers, got his shoes and set his things in the sun to dry.

"I always think of Bo Derek in Tarzan when I see a man in his underwear roaming the jungle." She chuckled.

"Wish I looked that good." He curled his arms and his bi-ceps bowed.

"Me too." She laughed.

"Ouch," he let his arms drop to his sides. "Great weight loss program here though."

"Yeah," she looked at the coconut trees. "So, you think that the sign on the tree is this tea trading company."

"I do," he got dressed. "I wonder how far south the pilot turned."

"If we're near the Bahamas, that's good for us, right?" She got her sandals on.

"No, that's way south of Atlanta." He looked at the trees across the stream. "I think we're mid-Atlantic, maybe nearer Bermuda before …"

"We crashed." She got up and looked herself over. "No more disgusting things on me." They made their way back to the beach. "Gosh, I'm hungry."

Bill chuckled.

"What's so funny?" She walked past him.

"Just us getting along." He looked up and down the beach. "I'd like to have laid that raft out."

She frowned, "Sorry, but …"

"No need, let's make an SOS out of coconuts on the beach." He looked around. "Got to be plenty."

Bill dragged his foot in the sand and that made a line that formed a big SOS.

They gathered coconuts and set them in the rows. The time past by as lazily as the waves lapping up the beach.

Bill used the Swiss Army knife to carve the end of a stick into a spear.

"Matches in the trunk." He was in the water, in his boxers. For an hour or so, he roamed the water hip deep and then shoved the spear down! "Got one!" He got a fire going and used the spear to hold the fish over the fire.

"Lemon and some dinnerware would be nice." Claire said and held the fish meat in her hands.

"Don't ruin the experience." Bill said and ate up the rest of the fish.

"Just making fun." She looked at the beach. "Do you think they'll find us?"

Bill looked at the cool blue ocean in front of them. "Yeah, I do." He looked at the radio. "Judas Priest, we never turned the radio on."

"You were sick, the fight and then …"

"Me in the rum pit and us drunk." He sat back. "Wow," he shook his head.

"Wow is right." She picked at a bone. "I want to go home."

Bill sighed, "yeah, me too."

"You sound hesitant." She sat up, got a strip of her ruined Dior and wiped her mouth. "Makes a really nice serviette."

"Sorry, you had to tear up your di-ore." He had a piece and wiped his mouth.

"Dior and I wasn't about to put a vomit ridden blouse back on." She scoffed. "The clean parts are fine."

"Suppose so," Bill looked up. "I'm not hesitant to be saved, but I want to …"

"Explore." She looked at the jungle.

He ate up and nodded.

"Even if they hear that thing, it'll be hours before a ship gets here." She wiped her hands on the Dior.

"Be a memento," he dipped his head at the blouse with the vomit.

"Dior Haute Couture, spring collection, with vomit on one side and cooked fish on the back?" She pursed her lips, "no."

He stood and got his shirt and jeans on. Then, he got the radio out and read the back of it. "Says here that this radio … not really a radio; it's an emergency position indicator radio beacon." He used his finger to follow the small print, "battery life may be reduced significantly when in use." He looked at Claire. "Guess, turn it on and then head back to the rum pit."

"Rum pit … you learn that on Discovery?" She waved her hands at a bug.

"NatGeo," he said.

"My son … he really enjoyed that show." She looked at the sand. "I … I'll be honest with you. I don't like the jungle at all and to go, to go back there with you …"

"Brings back some bad feelings?" Bill stepped up to her. "Would your son want you to go?"

She jerked her head up and they locked eyes. Her face warmed and then she bit at her lip. "Yes, I believe he would want me to go." Tears welled up in her eyes.

"Don't let them beat you." Bill smiled warmly.

"Who?" She turned to get up.

He held out his hand. "Those terrible feelings about what happened."

She looked at his hand and then her luggage where her son's picture rested. She turned back to Bill and slowly held up her hand.

"You want to bring him along?" Bill helped her up and then gave her the spear.

"No, I … I think it's time I went on my own." She got the spear. "You want me to defend you?"

"No," he chuckled. "You can use it as a walking stick."

They looked at each other and grinned. Then, Bill turned the radio on and set it by their things. He got the water and they walked into the jungle. It wasn't long and they crossed the stream, refilled their water and then stopped at the tree.

"So, here the adventure begins." Bill said and looked at Claire, "you ready?"

She forced a smile, "no, but let's see how it plays out."

"Mary Read or Anne Bonny," he said.

"Who are Mary Read and Anne Bonny?" She asked and rolled her eyes.

Chapter 8: Mary Read and Anne Bonny

"Pirates," Bill said and winked at her.

Claire laughed, "Really?"

"Yep, they're also characters in a game called, 'Assassin's Creed.'"

"Not a very nice name for a game." She lost her footing, but used the stick to get it back. "Thanks for the stick."

"Welcome," he looked ahead. "No, but it's a cool game." He looked at the jungle: small brush, coconut trees, sticker grass and sand. "How old was your son?"

She took a deep breath. To talk about Mark sent her anxiety through the roof. She cleared her throat. "Fifteen."

"Did he play Xbox?" Bill looked back at her.

She caught her breath. "I ... it's not easy for me to talk about him, not yet."

"Sorry," he pushed through the brush and moved a fallen palm frond out of the way. "These things are huge."

She smiled and wound her way around the fallen branch.

The birds chirped and cawed.

"Funny, we're surrounded by the Atlantic Ocean and can't hear it." He looked behind him.

"Funny," her sun burned skin cooled and paled. "So, Mary Read was a pirate?"

"A pirate who became a privateer," he looked ahead. "Could swear that pit was here."

She looked around. "What are you looking for?"

"That rum pit." He pointed.

"Johnny Depp will leap out any minute now." She laughed.

"Mary Read was a real pirate." He wiped the sweat from his brow and felt the cut to his head.

"A woman as a pirate, not something I could pull off." She dabbed a piece of ripped Dior to her head.

"She dressed as a man." Bill turned and looked Claire over.

Claire hesitated to say it, "What do you do with all that stuff tucked into your head?" She looked at the jungle and swallowed hard. "Doesn't it make you crazy?"

"No, I just have diverse interest." He walked off. "Must be this way."

"Is that what they call it?" She laughed.

"Don't let the devil possess you again." He turned and pointed his finger at her. "I *am* a jack of all trades."

"And who was Anne Bonny?" She stumbled on some broken limbs. "Damn it."

"Just another pirate that was a woman." He helped her up.

"Okay," a sand crab darted across her path. "Oh!"

"What?"

"Little scorpion or something just ran across here." She stepped back and aimed her walking stick.

"Probably a sand crab." He looked around. "They're harmless."

"Is there anything you don't know?" She jabbed the stick into some brush.

"Yeah, where the buried treasure is." His smile was as wide as his face.

She smirked, "Surely, you don't believe there's treasure out here."

He stopped and turned to her. "I don't know, but I want to find out."

"Diverse interest?" She stopped and caught her breath. "And master of none?"

"My grandma said that to me a lot, that I'm a jack of all trades and a master of none." He looked around some brush. "She was sarcastic when she said it and it used to …"

"Make you mad?" She walked on. "Grandma's worry, my grandma always worried about me and kept after me if I didn't behave properly."

"I get annoyed with her." He looked up a tree. "Need some more signs."

"She's alive then?" She wiped the sweat from her brow. "So humid."

"Yeah, she lives in Paris." Bill looked past a dune. "Just past that dune."

"Lives in Paris, okay." Claire looked at the trees. "Jungle's thicker, darker now."

Bill looked around, "Yeah, maybe."

"So, you speak French?"

"My French sucks." He laughed, "And that really annoys her."

"Mine's not very good, but I have a PA that travels with me when I visit." She looked over the dune. "I think we're close to your rum pit."

"Why were you in Paris?" Bill stopped and looked on the other side of the dune.

She hesitated and sighed. "My son … it was his favorite place."

"Ah, there's the rum pit, the rum and the rope." He looked the things over. "Here we go."

Claire looked on with a curious expression. "Go where."

He looked at her and found her question odd or out of place. "Go look for the treasure."

"How do you even know there is any treasure?" She pursed her lips in disbelief.

"Mary Read and Anne Bonny, pirates hide their booty." He said.

"And their names are on the rum?" She looked the crates over. "I'd say the rum is worth something."

"No, not both names, but the initials, M.R." He wiped the sand and grit from the top of a crate.

"Seems like a mad plan to pursue, I mean you're guessing at all of it, aren't you?" She walked over and ran her hand over the initials, "could be Mark, or Mike or …"

"Don't ruin the fun." He grinned slyly. "Don't you want half?"

"Good God, that's what my lawyer asked me and it was my money." She shook her head. "My stomach isn't having fun." She looked at the trees. "Coconut's juice is nutritious."

"Yeah, it is." He looked the crates over and then looked in the pit. "I'm going back in."

"What!" She felt her heart pound against her chest. "Why?"

"What's on top may sometimes be a trick." He got the rope in hand and pulled on it. "See, they put the rum in there and figure if someone finds it why look further?"

"Yeah, why are you looking further?" She made a worrisome sigh.

He squinted at her. "Because, what's the alternative?" He looked at the pit. "We go sit on the beach, build a hut and wait for rescue?"

She smiled, "yes, I happen to like that idea!"

"Boring!" He got the rope, got his legs on the edge and lowered himself inside. "Boring."

"I like boring; boring is safe." She went to the edge and looked over. "Safe!"

He lowered himself down and pushed off the side, dropped, pushed off the side, dropped and then hit the bottom. "Don't remember it being this deep."

"Well, it is that deep and you're down there." She felt a surge of worry overtake her and mumbled, "Be safe."

He looked around the pit. "They've got the sides held up with wood planks and rocks in-between them." His eyes went over every board. Every board had a cross symbol with a number four at the top or what looked like the number four. "The boards have the same mark that's on the tree."

"Look closer, maybe they'll have a sticky note or something that says, buried treasure – dig here." She laughed.

"Ha-ha," he got to one board with the symbol, but the smaller letters in the cross were different. "Here we go."

"What?"

He got his fingers into the edges around the board and tried to pry it loose. "Can't get my fingers," he got the pocket knife out and dug at the edges.

"Maybe you should wrap the rope around you." She got the rope and swung it towards him.

"I'm alright." He pushed the blade in deep and drew it down the side of the board. Then, he did the same on the other side of the board. "Just want to get this board loose."

She pulled the rope up and then flung it at him. The rope whipped up and popped him on his back!

"Owe!" He jerked his head back. "What the hell?"

"Sorry, I want you to have the rope." She flung it around again.

"You wanted me to be safe and then you used the rope to whip me." He snatched it and set it to the side of the board.

"Sorry," she sat back and looked at him. "Just, why don't you at least have it … I don't know, in your hand?"

"You don't know." He snapped and wiped the heavy line of sweat from his brow. "Just," a sigh pushed through his lips. "I'll be alright."

"Sorry," she pursed her lips, looked up and muttered the words, "please watch over him." Then, she looked back, "more than you did my son."

"Damn board." He had the blade stuck between the two boards and pried. The board moved just a tiny bit. "It's moving."

"That's what I'm afraid of." She looked on and her hands wrenched over one another.

"It's fine." He said firmly and his fingers picked away at the edges. Then, he got a couple fingers in the board and pulled back! The board popped out and hit him in the face.

"Oh my God, are you ..."

"Fine!" He set the board to the side and then rubbed his face. "Damn, that hurt."

She looked at him and the rope. The rope was a foot or so away from him. She wanted to put it closer to him, but didn't want to whip him again. "The rope, it's just …"

He looked at her and dipped his chin. "I know you're being helpful and the rope is right there."

"Okay," she tried to smile in a happy way, but her worrisome smile took its place.

There was another board behind the one he set aside with big initials carved into it, "M.R." He ran his hand over the initials to get the sand off. "See, M.R., Mary Read."

She mumbled, "or most ridiculous."

"I heard that." The board under the one he popped off was smooth and had a cutout for a person to get their hand into. He looked in the cutout and a little bit of wind pushed out. "Think there's something behind here, behind this board."

"You know that movie Jurassic Park?" Claire looked around.
"Yeah," Bill turned to her and put his hands on his hips. "Go ahead."

"Maybe there's a velo-raptor thing, you know … like a monster behind there." She showed her teeth!

He shook his head and realized she had a reason to worry, her son. "I know you're worried." He licked the dryness from his lips. "But, I'm okay."

"Okay," she pursed her lips and looked at the jungle. "I'm not very strong."
He got his fingers in the cutout and pulled up. The board came right up! Then, the ground rumbled! Bill looked at the rope. The sand beneath him disappeared into cracks that got bigger and then the floor fell away! "AH!" He reached for the rope!

"Bill!" She sat up and grabbed the rope. "BILL!"

Everything beneath him fell into deeper pit. Jagged stakes lined the ground below and their pointed ends aimed at whoever may fall on them. "Damn the luck!" He clung to the side of the pit and looked at the board. "I'm alright." He caught his breath and wiped his face off.

She put her hand to her chest, "give me a heart attack."

"Nearly gave me one." He looked into the hole. "There was a rope hooked to the back of that board that triggered a trap door."

"I hear you, Indiana." She wiped the nervous sweat from her brow.

"Ha-ha," he balanced himself against the wall, leaned over and moved the board.

"That's it, move it some more and maybe a monster will come eat you." She clicked her teeth.

He smiled, "Can't hear you." His fingers played with the edges of the board.

"Bill, why not just let it go?" She pulled at the rope. "Just come up." Her heart beat frantically!

"No, hang on. I just want to see what's behind here." He pushed the board with his fingers and saw something. "There's a box on the back of the board."

"Far dem er temps gefar." She looked up and had her arms out, palms up.

"What!" He picked at the box to get it loose.

"For this, you temp danger?" She looked around her. "Stop tempting danger … and where's the water?"

"By you," he didn't take his eyes from the box. "Got it!" The lid opened and a pouch made of leather fell out. "HEY!" He grabbed it just before it fell to the stakes below. He leaned over and looked in the crevice behind the board. "That's it." The rolled leather was bigger than his hand and longer than his forearm. "Got to be." He swung to the side and climbed up.

"Are you coming out now?" She looked over and Bill was there. Her skin cooled and her heart slowed its worrisome beat.

"Hey," he smiled, pulled himself up and out and rolled onto his back. "Think it's a map."

Chapter 9: The Map of M.R.

Bill fought to catch his breath and held the pouch tightly. His knuckles were nearly white from the grip he had on the leather.

"We need food." She looked him over and shook her head. "I know that this means something to you." She touched the very tip of the leather pouch.

He looked at her as she hovered over him. "It does mean something to me." His stomach growled loud enough that the birds stopped their cries and wondered what made that sound. He looked at his stomach. "Let me look at it first."

"Of course," she knelt by him.

He looked at the pouch and there was a thick leather string around it. The leather was rough, dark and cracked in places. His fingers worked quickly to undo the double bowtie string and get to the meat of it. "C'mon," he fidgeted to get the second knot undone, but the wet, heat and time had tightened it up.

"You have that pocket knife, just cut it." The birds cawed wildly.

He looked at her and got the knife. "Right." In the blink of an eye, the knife went through the leather tie and that was that. The leather flap gave way, but did not open up entirely to reveal its secrets.

"Alright, I'm a little excited about this, but if I see 'Made in China' on it … I'm going to kick your …" She patted his shoulder.

"I get it." His fingers gently worked their way into the edge of the flap leather. "It's all leather."

"Chinese make stuff from leather." She said.

"Don't let evil possess you." He studied the rough-cut edge, lifted it up and unfolded the flap. "Okay," he flipped the flap over. "Oh, it's a …"

"Pouch, nice one too." She looked it over. "Chinese make …"

"*Don't.*" He said firmly. The pocket opened and there was a parchment inside the pouch nearly the length of the pouch. "Oh, wow." He got his fingertips on the parchment and pulled it out slowly.

"When we're done, can we figure out something for lunch?" She asked and looked around the jungle. "Feels like we're being watched."

Bill jolted himself from the parchment when he heard that and looked around too. "Just the jungle, it has that effect on people." He rubbed his fingers on the leather. "A leather letter?"

"Nice," she touched it.

He got the letter from the pouch and set the pouch in his lap. "It is leather." There was a wax seal and a firm impression in the wax. "Same symbol from the tree."

"And that means?" She rolled her eyes.

"Means whoever marked the tree marked the pouch." He ran his fingers along the edge of the letter.

"And put the deadly stakes in the ground that were waiting for you." She chuckled.

"Waiting for anyone that wasn't happy with the rum." He looked around.

"See, I was happy with the rum." She looked at the jungle and the birds cawed.

"I wonder if Johnny Depp will come for the rum." He laughed. "Be cool if he did."

"Be even better if he had some foie gras and wine." She rubbed her stomach again.

"Foie gras is gross, fat duck liver, blah." He pried at the wax seal that held the letter shut. "Alright, I know I want to see what's inside." His fingers rested on the wax seal.

"It probably says you've won the Publishers Clearing House giveaway." She got up and walked to the side of the pit.

"She who laughs first." Bill said and got his pocketknife. He pushed the blade through the wax.

"May not prevail in the end." She said and was rather smug about it. "Bet you didn't know that."

"I didn't." He cut through the seal. "Thank God, you're here."

"Don't be evil, jack." She walked back and rubbed her stomach. "After you look at …"

"Jack?" He shook his head. "Jack Sparrow?"

"No, jack of all trades." She said.

"THUMP!" A coconut fell nearby.

"Ah!" She jumped!

"Just a coconut," he unfolded the edge. "Okay," there were three folds and the letter opened. "Looks like old English script with lots of fancy curved letters and double lines for capitals." There was a red "N" at the top that was outlined in black ink; the red ink was faded. The leather letter was ragged, dried and somewhat brittle. "Letter's seen better days." He gently held it up to the sun that was on its way down. "Oh, wow."

"What?" She knelt right by him.

"Mark Read," Bill began and read on. "By the grace of God, King of England, Scotland, and Ireland, defender of the faith. To our trust and well-beloved Mark Read," he read on silently and then looked at Claire.

"Mark? I thought you said Mary." She tilted the letter so that she could see it.

"Mark is Mary." He said and looked at the letter. "She was put to everyone as a boy and lived as a man, Mark Read."

"I have gay friends who say stuff like that, Mark was Mary, Mary is Mark." Claire shook her head. "So, you're saying that this Mark Read was really Mary Read."

Bill's eyes could have burned a hole in her skin. "Yes, she got a commission to privateer after she was arrested as a pirate." He said and looked the letter over. "Some funny stuff on the letter though."
"Like food particles?"

"Okay, we'll stop for now, get some food and stop your moaning." He folded the letter, put it in the leather pouch and folded the flap back over. "But, if there's a waiting coast guard ship, I'm heading back here."

"Have a nice treasure hunt then, because I'm leaving for a hot shower, hot food and a manicure and pedicure." She walked ahead of him back to the beach.

Bill had the spear and walked the shallows in his briefs.

She shouted from up the beach. "You have a thing about walking around in your briefs!"

"Yes, I love it." He said and did a muscle man pose. "Makes me feel right about myself."

She put her hand up and moved some rocks around a fire. "Thank you, but that's quite enough information."

"You asked." He focused at a fish that moved around his feet.

"And I'm so sorry that I did." She laughed, "Men."

"Rich, uptight women," he said and thrust the spear down. The spear jiggled and shook. "Got one!"

"Uh-huh."

The fish was gone in minutes along with most of their water.

Bill looked in the water pouch and at her water bottle. "We're nearly out."

"Thank you for dinner," she said and dipped her head at him.

"You're welcome, Queen of New York and this island." He laughed.

She laughed, "I wish." She looked back at the jungle and then at Bill. "I, can we make something to sleep on or have some, I don't know … shelter?"

"Hut?" He grinned, "see what I can get worked out."

She rubbed her leg. "Thank you."

He got up and took the knife out. "Jack of all trades."

"More like a master of them." She turned and watched his butt jiggle through his briefs. "Uh, you could put some clothes on."

"I could." He disappeared among the coconut trees and brush.

"Men," she chuckled.

That evening, Bill had a lean two built that was roomy enough for both of them. "How about that?"

"Nice as my cottage in Newport." She said and looked at the collection of boards, vine and palm fronds. "Will it keep the bugs out?"

"No, be lucky if it keeps the rain out." He said and got a few boards across the front. "I checked the radio and it's still sending a signal or at least that's what it says."

"But," she said and looked him over.

"But, I want to go back. I …"

"What is it about that letter?" She was a little annoyed. "I mean that's all it is. We both saw it and there wasn't a map on it."

"No, but there were some funny symbols and I want to look at them." He said firmly.

"Bill, we have to get off this island. I want … we should do what we can to signal for help and go home." She went through her luggage. "Another night," she muttered.

He felt his face warm up. Even with the sun nearly gone and cool breezes coasting off the ocean to them, he was hot. "Okay, I know that and you've said it enough."

She sighed quietly, went to the lean-two and set her things out.

He took the letter from the pouch and read it with the glow from the fire. The "N" at the top seemed odd to him and he looked the letter over for other odd things. Then, he saw the line in the firelight that led from certain letters to certain letters. "And we do hereby enjoin you to keep an exact journal of your proceedings in executions of the premises." His eyes locked on the "x" in execution; it was much larger than the other letters. The lines from some letters all ended at the "X", "where x marks the spot."

She overheard him. "Bill, in all seriousness, you don't believe that they really have an 'X' on some spot on the island." She pursed her lips in frustration.

"No, I don't." He looked at the half moon. "But, I do believe that the X in this letter marks a spot somewhere on this island where ..."

"Buried treasure waits." She finished.

He wiped the sweat from his brow. "I'm going for a walk." He got up and headed down the beach.

"Isn't it a little too dark?" She looked at the jungle.

Morning came and the sun crested the ocean. Bill was asleep on the sand with his jeans rolled up under his head. His tan was the darkest he'd ever known and his hair finally gave in and began to turn to a pale yellow.

Claire's cheeks were darker than they'd ever been without rouge from Yves Saint Laurent to brighten them up. The sun beat on her lips and the lip balm was no longer helpful. Little bits of skin peeled up from her dry lips, cheeks and the very tip of her nose. She coughed, woke and looked at Bill.

Bill turned and half his face had sand on it. His lips were cracked and his face was nearly as rough looking as that leather pouch that was buried behind a board for nearly three hundred years. His tongue poked out and tried to comfort his lips with a soft lick, but that wasn't enough.

She sat up and looked at the ocean. "Normally, I'd wake and love that view."

Bill yawned and sucked up some sand. He coughed and hacked, "damn!" The sand coated his tongue and throat. "Damn sand," he spat and looked for the water. "Water," he got the water sack and rinsed his mouth out.

She looked him over and moved her jaw to say something, but nothing came out. It was time; they had to do more to signal for help or get off the island. She didn't even know how long they'd been on the island, a few days, a couple weeks or a month. "Bill," she edged up and got the lip balm out.

"What?" He rubbed the sleep from his eyes.

She squeezed a tiny dot of balm onto her finger and rubbed it over her lip. "We really need to think about getting off the island or figuring some other way to signal for help."

He huffed, got his jeans on and got the pouch. "What is it with you?"

"What do you mean?" Her brow went up.

He smirked, looked at the ocean and then turned to her. "Movies show people leave an island and float around until they're rescued."

"Okay," she looked through her things. "Sounds good."

"That's movies." He pointed at the jungle. "Remember the shark, the lack of water, food … I mean how long do you think we'll last floating around out there."

She felt a surge of emotion at the back of her throat. She was going to vomit, but it wouldn't be rum. "I don't want to spend my remaining days stuck here."

"Okay, so go." He had the pouch and the water in hand. "We have food, water, and shelter here."

"Oh, so that's it then and you'll go look for buried treasure to pass the time." She got up and dusted herself off.

"Better than sitting here listening to your broken record." His face warmed and he felt something at the back of his throat pushing itself up too, an urge to argue.

"Look, I … I appreciate what you've done, but hunting for treasure is stupid!" She put her hands on her hips.

"Shouldn't put your hands on your hips, honey." He chuckled. "That's how I got started."

"What is it with you people!" She pointed at him. "Being rescued is reality, going treasure hunting is fantasy!"

"Here we go with the people thing. Spend more time being less hateful." Then, the angry words at the back of his throat pulsed.

"I'm not hateful!" She felt the heat from her face, the anger that stormed in her heart right along with the fear that she might actually be stuck on an island, this island. "I said you people, because that's the way it is with *you people*! You just can't deal with reality, with real work, or with life!" The words vomited. "On and on you go about how bad you have it, how hard you have it, and how things are always wrong for you. Get over it and get on with it!"

Bill inhaled deep. He felt the urge to scream, to bury her in horrible words and bad feelings, but he let the anger out slowly through pursed lips. "Go to hell." He got the spear, the knife, a water pack, the leather pouch, and headed into the jungle, "whatever I complain about at least I don't take my hurt out on others."

"You go to hell!" She screamed and nearly threw her throat out with the last words. "GO TO HELL!"

Bill was deep in the jungle in minutes. His feet made easy work of the sand trail and, suddenly, there were cawing birds, coconut trees and brush around him.

Claire looked around her; there was the sun, the beach, the jungle and the lean two with her things underneath the boards and palm fronds. Then, a tear slid down her cheek. "What am I going to do?" She brought her hands up to her face and cried.

Bill sat down, set the spear down and got the letter out. He looked at the letter and studied the "N" at the top. "I'll be damn, north." He looked around, "has to be north." He oriented the map and then turned to the rising sun. "East, okay." The map was on the sand and 'N' pointed north. His eyes followed the lines, "but where's start?" He looked over every word, "the rum pit, so R?" His eyes keenly scanned each word. "God, there's like a hundred R's in this letter." He started over and read on. "Okay, authority to apprehend, seize or take into your custody," he put his fingertip right to the word and then read on. "blah, blah, John Ireland," he sighed. "C'mon, give me a little help ... their ships and vessels and all such merchandises, money, goods, *rum* and wares." He smiled, "HA!" He put his finger on the word, "rum" and followed the line from it upwards to "mariners." "What's M stand for?" Some letters were underlined, "Oh big duh, Mary ... 'M', rum ... Read.'" He panned the jungle and saw darkness behind the trees ahead of him where "mariners" were located on the map. "Sounds too easy, but I'm going with it." He got the spear, got up and walked with passion and conviction into the darkness ahead of him. The birds cawed and screamed as his body faded into the jungle's jaws and then the jungle closed over him.

Claire wiped the tears away. "Can't just sit here and cry." She got up and looked over the beach. "I'm not beaten, not here and damn well not now." She straightened her Dior blouse and got her sandals on. Then, she checked herself in a small hand mirror. "Oh my God!" She studied her rough red skin, the deep-burned creases and the crow's feet at the corners of her eyes. She hurriedly went through a cosmetic kit and found blush and some tubes of Kiehls, "yes, Kiehls!" She opened the blush and water came out. "Oh no, no, no." The blush was more sludge like and creeped towards the end pointed at the ground. "Hundred and forty-five dollars ... water resistant my ..." She tossed it back in the cosmetic bag. Then, she got the Kiehls open and it was a fine white cream. "There ya go," she got some around her eyes and then over her cheeks. "They need an island version." She looked at the tube's fine print. "One point five ounces, really I need a pound." The cream soaked in and eased the burns. She packed it all back up and then looked around. "See what we can find, but first I need water .... No, perfume." She got the bottle of Annick Goutal, Eau D'Hadrien. She spritzed herself on the wrist and neck, then turned and went into the jungle. "I'll be damned if they find my corpse with rotted skin on bones dressed in Dior couture and smelling like a dead person." She shook off the image. "Water's at the stream." She got her bottle.

Bill fell again and got himself up. The spear didn't work as well as a walking stick for him. He pressed on into the jungle. The jungle's canopy was thick and the fresh air above it would never reach him down here. Sweat sat on his brow, heavy, and each wipe only made room for more sweat. "Claire," he said and gritted his teeth. "She could have come, but no, she wants to wait for a rescue." He spat and stopped. He drank and the water washed over his mouth and tongue to quench an insatiable thirst; every drop of sweat took water from him and he knew he had to have more water soon, but the bottle *was* half-empty. Trees and brush, everywhere he looked it was thick with trees and brush.

He stopped at a cluster of coconut trees and looked around. "I'm going through." He climbed up and over and then stopped when he saw the mangroves. His feet cried out when they hit stagnant water. "Oh damn," it was a field of mangroves ahead of him, roots sprouted from one mangrove to another mangrove, hundreds of them were tied into others. "Okay, that's a lot of mangroves." He looked left and then right. "Of course, there's no other way through … right Mary?" He looked at the map. "Mariners with a line right through here, has to be. You nearly killed me just for this map, so I know there's something you're protecting."

Claire was in the jungle. "Bill!" She looked around. "I should have gone with him." Her sandals went into the sand and then she struggled to get them out. "Sand," she kicked her foot. "Just go barefoot." She took the sandals off and got them in her hand. "Keep an eye out for stickers." She looked around the ground.

Bill rolled the leather parchment and then tucked it into his back pocket. He stepped carefully from one root to another root. He looked behind him and the jungle faded into the mangrove where their boundaries met and one did not encroach on the other. "God, it stinks … brackish water or stale water."

Every mangrove root was slick, lumpy and curved down into the dark water beneath it. Little things darted around the roots, small fish, crabs, shrimp and unknown critters. From the roots up, there were brown branches that bent like bows and had little knots all over them; they had dark green leaves at the ends of their branches that clouded out the sun and fresh air.

He placed his foot firmly on the next root, grasped a mangrove branch and pulled himself up and over to the next root. "Remember, you're looking for pirate treasure. They're not going to just set it out and say, 'here.'" He drove the spear in-between some roots to have a kind of rail to use.

Something growled in the shadows and Bill jumped! "What the?" He held the spear towards the sound.

"Bill!" Claire looked around the stream and filled her water bottle. She had another pouch and filled it too. "Bill?" Her dark tan lightened with worry. She bit at her bottom lip and then took a drink. "Uh," she coughed. "How did the natives ever get by drinking this stuff?"

Bill did his best to see around the mangroves, but their branches and roots locked into each other. Drops of sweat slid around his eyes and the heat was nearly intolerable. "Gets any hotter, I'm going to have to head back." Then, he shook his head. "No, I'm not." He drew his arm across his

123

forehead, wiped away the wet and then looked at everything again. "No crocs in mangroves, maybe it's Claire." He laughed to himself, reached out and got his fingers around another branch, pulled up, placed his foot and then stepped over. "Man," his nose bucked the stench. "Smells like day old poop." He blew his nose. "Been in stagnant mangroves in the Florida Keys and they didn't smell this bad." The mangrove canopy had the sun nearly blocked out; some strands of orange got through the canopy and made a spot here or there brighter. He stopped and squinted. Something changed across his path. "What was that?" His hand went up and out into the shadows. "What the …" He reached a little further and his hand bumped something very thin, very taught. "What the?" He got his foot on another root and then used his other hand to pull him over to what hung in the air. He gently placed his hand on it. "String?" He looked up and down. Then, he moved his hand lower. "Another string," he pulled his hand back and lowered it, "and another." His feet fought to keep themselves steadied on the slick root.

"Bill?" She looked around on the other side of the stream, nothing. The sun was overhead and her stomach growled. "I'd eat a non-organic hamburger right now."

Bill studied the strings that ran across his path. He looked to the left and right, more string. "Ah!" His foot slipped, his hand naturally reached out, his fingers caught the string and pulled it down with him. The spear slid off the root, into the water and was gone!

Several arrows shot through the air at the spot where Bill fell into the water! One shot right past his face and cut the edge of his nose, "Da …!" Water bubbled up in his mouth.

Claire headed back to the beach and was across the stream. She had her sandals in hand and the water in her other hand. "Hope nothing happened to him," she stopped, looked back and then up. The sun was past the noon hour and she felt her heart give way to worry. Her face cooled and she caught her breath. "Bill," she muttered and then headed back to the beach.

Bill popped up and his mouth burst open for air! He floated and got hold of the root nearest him. His hands trembled and grabbed the root with a grip strong enough to snap the root in two. "Damn it!" He brought his legs up and hurried to get out the water. "Damn, I hate dark water!" Just as he climbed up, he saw a string inches from his face. His hand missed it when he reached up. "Oh damn." He licked the water from his lips, "Okay, that's totally gross." He spat. The string was just below several others that crisscrossed over his head. "Son of a ..." He felt his nose and there was some blood. He looked down, "I hate when I can't see what's under me." He closed his eyes. "Gonna have to swim or get shot with arrows ... conquer your fear." He shook his head. "I call bull shi ..."

Claire was at the lean-two and got her things together. She looked around the lean-two and then walked around it. "What did he do with it?" She put her hands on her hips. "Bill!" She shouted at the jungle. "Bill, where the hell is the spear!"

The birds and other critters yelled back!

Bill wanted to be sure about the booby traps, so he reached out, put just the tips of his fingers on another line of string and sank lower into the water. "Some kind of twine." Then, he took a breath and pulled on the twine! He was under water when an arrow shot past! He floated up and slowly came out of the water just enough to look at the other twine. "Guess I am going to try and conquer my fear of being in the water." He floated under the twine and drifted deeper into the maze of mangroves. "Or take a chance and get shot with an arrow … the map, crap!" He reached back and got the leather pouch from his pocket.

"Bill!" Claire yelled. The wind picked up and shoved her back. She looked at the ocean and dark clouds were heavy on the horizon. "Oh, no." The wind shoved her again. "Where are you, Bill?" She hurried to her things and got them under the lean two. Then, she set the luggage in-between her and the ocean. "God, don't make it a bad storm."

He held the pouch in his hand as he drifted under another set of twine. "Getting close, ain't that right Mary?" He looked at the twine that crisscrossed in different spots. Dew clung to his face and no amount of swipes with his forearm would get it all off. He sighed and tempted fate; he slowly tilted his head to look into the water. His lips jiggled and his head trembled, "I hate when I can't see the bottom … breathe." He pursed his lips and let his breath out slowly. "Calm down," the water was far too dark to see a thing. His feet begged his legs to kneel and keep them from the depths. Then, a mosquito bit him. "Ah!" He slapped it. "Damn dirty things."

Then, another mosquito bit him and another landed on him for blood! He swiped and went under. He came back up and there were little black dots all over! "Oh no," he swiped his hands over and over! "Got to get out of here!" He kicked at the water and his hands lunged out, grabbed mangrove roots and pulled him away in sudden jerks. "AH!" Hundreds of little mosquitoes attacked him! They bit him all over his neck, hands and face. Any skin was a target for the blood thirsty little savages!

Claire studied the trunk with a careful eye and waited, "Bill, I hope you're okay."

Bill thrashed at the water and hurried ahead, but the mangroves were a knotted mess of roots and branches. To get through them was much like trying to get through a bunch of fish nets. "Ah!" He slapped his neck, his cheeks and his forehead. "Damn things!" His legs kicked and splashed the water!

Finally, Bill was some distance from the blood sucking devils. He shook terribly. "Not what I needed." Despite the melee of his hands swinging wildly at the mosquitoes, it was apparent that some had bitten him; little red spots swelled all over him. He caught his breath and looked up. "Now what?"

"Dark up and dark down," His face cooled and goose bumps popped up all over him. "Chills, great ... nothing scarier than to be in the water, in the dark with booby traps over me." Then, he chuckled, "no, scarier when that shark had the rope and pulled me to the water while Claire was clueless; that was scary." He smiled and moved through the roots and under the twine. "She's scary," he chuckled. "And now little black devil bugs sucked the blood from me ... this sucks."

Claire looked at the waves that were higher, white capped and crashed onto the beach. "Bill, where are you?" Thunderclouds moved slowly towards the tiny island and jolts of lightning shot through them. Winds buffeted the tiny lean-two, the palm fronds rattled and shifted; it was a rickety house staring down a tornado!

She pulled the windbreaker hoodie on her head and wiped the rain from her face. "Mark, this storm scares me."

The sun was gone now and the thunder roared overhead! Lightning spanked the clouds and cracked its whip!

She edged back to a corner and covered her face. Her stomach rumbled. "No fish tonight," she patted her belly.

The raindrops tapped the leaves over Bill's head. Lightning whipped the air and it sizzled with static! He stopped and looked around him. "Biggest bathtub I've ever been in and a lightning storm raging over me." He pulled up onto a mangrove root and looked around. There, just in front of him, were more booby-trapped lines. Though the twine wasn't as tightly pulled as the others, it still meant that there was an arrow waiting for a fool. He closed his eyes tight and thought about options: crawl through the twine, stay in one place out of the water, keep swimming and hope the lightning passes without shocking him or go back. "I ain't going back." He said firmly. He opened his eyes and looked at the darkness ahead of him. Then, he sighed heavy, "Can't see the twine in this darkness."

The wind chewed and bit the lean-two, but it held. Claire looked past a slit in the hoodie and the rain slapped her face. Bill tied the palm fronds to the frame, so they held well. She trembled and with every thunderclap. "Mark!" She got his picture and held it close.

Bill crawled onto the roots. He settled in just below some twine that was strung across and over his head. "Just rest for now," he said. The map was soaked, but the leather was sturdy. He laid it on a root to dry out, "better than paper." Then, he used the knife to mark his direction, "headed that way." He leaned back on the mangrove roots, but they were unforgiving as a bed. He turned and tried to find a way to lie across them comfortably if any person could lie comfortably across a bed made of hard roots. Finally, he got himself propped up against a larger mangrove. "Now, just rest until," but he never finished the next word. His eyes fell shut. The rain slapped the leaves above him and lightning cracked the clouds, air and ground.

The next morning, Claire lay under a pile of palm fronds, boards and sand. The storm beat the lean-two to death. She tried to sit up and then she felt the weight of those things on her! "Hey," she pushed up and then kicked! "HEY!" Palm fronds, boards and a branch flew off her! "Get off of me!" She kicked and punched at the debris! Dior and other name brands got smacked down in the fray! "AH!" She screamed and burst through the junk! She leapt up and then pushed out onto the beach, "What the hell happened?" That fresh salt air cleared her sinuses and she inhaled deeply. "Help!" She screamed, "I want off this damned island!"

The beach had some branches and leaves scattered around. Claire shook her hair and felt the bits of sand. "Yuck," she turned and saw the lean-two. "Oh, damn." Her luggage and clothes were scattered around. "Damn, damn, damn." She got her things and shook the sand out of them. The wind gently ran up her back and the waves made odd sounds as they pushed up and into something, a clap sound that rung in her ears. "What is that?" She looked at the beach and her heart sank. "Oh … oh no."

There were pieces of the fuselage and personal belongings spread along the beach.

She covered her mouth and her eyes panned the beach from one end to the other. At the far end, something caught her eye and her heart beat again. "The raft?" She squinted and looked again. "The raft?" She walked towards it. "It's the raft!" She half-ran, half walked with her bad leg giving her some grief. "THE RAFT!" She was elated and broke into a cockeyed run with her leg dragging behind in a limp while her other leg was in a full out sprint! "Bill! The Raft is here!" She was nearly there!

The big yellow blob lifted up and then down with each gentle wave that rolled under it.

"Ha! It's waving at me!" She waved back. "I'm coming!" A bright, big smile blew up on her sun burnt face. "BILL!" She looked back once and hoped that he'd be there. "Oh my God, we have it!" She stopped just a few feet away from it. "How to get it up?" She looked the end over and was a little surprised. "Don't remember it being that full of air." She saw a handle. "Got to pull it up, get it on shore … Bill's going to be so happy!"

The raft bobbed up and then down with each wave. It was very much like the ocean wanted her to have the raft, because each wave pushed the raft further up onto the beach head.

"Okay, okay," she got hold of the handle, but that part of the raft was bunched up on itself. She pulled, her hand came loose and she fell backwards onto the sand. "Damn it." Her legs kicked right back up. The raft bunched up in a half fold so that the handle was turned into the raft. She looked over the end of the raft and then saw the handle bob up when a wave rolled under the raft. "Ah!" She got her hand firmly into the handle, got her other hand on it and pulled hard! "C'mon, you fat yellow …"

The raft gave in and flopped forward. It rolled up and into Claire. Then, something popped up and rolled onto the edge of the raft. Her eyes widened!

Chapter 10: Tell No Tales

"AH!" She screamed and threw her hands up! A man's rotted body flopped over the edge and right on top of her! "AH!" She screamed again and threw her hands up to knock him away!

The man's skin was greenish-black and waxy. Birds had eaten his eyeballs, parts of his cheeks and his lips away. His bowels flowed freely and the stench leapt onto Claire to get away from the rotting corpse!

She kicked and shoved her hands up to get him off her! "GET OFF!" The body lay flat against her and his arms fell to her sides. "GET OFF!" She turned over and he flopped onto her back. "AH!" She screamed again and pulled at the sand to get free! The rotted skin of his head lay flat against her neck. "AH!" Some sort of human stickiness slithered onto her. "AH!" Her hands dragged back huge piles of sand each time she reached out, but she couldn't get out from under him! The raft bucked, kicked, and then lurched forward onto the man's legs to hold him still so that she could get out from under him.

Claire dug her elbows in, brought her legs up and dug her feet in! Then, she pushed and was free! "AH!" She got up and shook horribly! "AH!" She turned and vomited what little was in her stomach. "Oh, God, oh God," she ripped her blouse off and ran her hands all over her chest and arms with handfuls of sand. She had to get the stench off of her and get the sticky mess off. "AH!" She screamed while her body jerked and jolted in shock.

The man's body flopped up and lay on the beach just ahead of the raft. The raft was, for the most part, on the beach and not going anywhere, nor was the man.

"Yuck, blah!" Then, tears bunched up in her eyes. She fell to the sand, looked at the raft and then at the man who fell on her. "Oh God," tears rolled down her dark cheeks, around her cracked lips and down her chin. Her stomach dry heaved over and over. "Bill … BILL!" She got more sand, rubbed it all over herself and tried to wash off the man's stench that stuck to her. "BILL!"

Bill was up and stretched hard. His muscles and bones ached. Some sunlight pierced the heavy-laden canopy of leaves and that's when the web of twine was visible. Across his path and for as far as he could see to his right and left, there was twine tied to branches and pulled tight. Arrows waited for unsuspecting victims. "What the hell." He rubbed the sleep from his eyes and looked at the twine. "All this … all this means there is something worth protecting."

He got his feet right and his body moaned in pain after it had lay on roots for most of the night. "Back in the water?" He looked at the murky depths and shadows. The pack had about half the water left, so he took a swig. "How bad do you want it?" He smiled, "I want it bad." His fingers quickly got the leather pouch and took it from his side, "keep you dry." The mark he made with his knife pointed where he had to go next, so he got his foot onto a root and then slowly slid down into the murky depths. "If you knew why I hated not seeing the bottom, you'd show me the bottom." The mangroves rose above him with sunlight that shot through tiny holes in the leafy canopy. The twine's web hung over him; it was a fishnet that wanted to trap him, wanted to kill him.

Claire wiped her eyes and shook off the terribleness of what happened. She looked at her blouse and thought to get it, but her nose wrinkled. "No, thank you." A quick turn and off she went off to the lean-two which was just flat on the ground. "My stuff," a moment later and her luggage was upright. There was the water bottle and she drank nearly all of it. She got her Dopp kit, marched off to the stream and looked around. "I know I saw him, but he isn't going to see me, no." She looked at every branch, leaf, coconut tree and blade of sand grass. "No surprises," and then she stripped. The water cooled her skin; she washed off nearly all of the dead body stench that was on her with her fancy perfume soap. Her fingers massaged her scalp and hair thoroughly with shampoo. She smelled her hands, "Oribe shampoo and then conditioner." She smelled the cap, "heaven."

The birds were quiet until they got a whiff of the shampoo. Then, they cawed so loudly that the noise echoed through the jungle and it warned the other birds to cover their nose!

"Don't be so jealous!" She shouted, "It's not made from birds." She looked the back of the bottle over, "at least I don't think it is."

Bill took a deep breath; then, he sighed and his anxiety went down. "Hate the water, but love the thought of treasure." His outstretched hands got hold of a root and he pulled himself ahead a few feet at a time. Slowly, he made his way through the mangrove swamp. Sweat beaded up on his forehead and gently made its way down the sides of his head where it paused on his cheeks. He shook and threw the sweat from his face, but all that did was make room for more. He stopped, turned his head slowly and looked back; his smile was halfhearted. The wind over the top of the mangroves rattled the leaves and startled him. He got the chill off him and moved on. "I hope it's not just like some more rum or bonds." He looked at the leafy canopy and then ahead at the many roots on either side of him. "They have bonds back then?" He shook his head and then stopped again. "Oh man," he reached up and touched his head. "That's just gross." His hair was dark, stringy and full of bits of dirt, bugs and oil. The salt air made it so his hair had a mushy feel to it. "Have to just shave it all off."

Claire was dressed in a lighter Dior blouse with clean capris. She dried her hair and smelled the ends of it. "So nice to be clean." Her Dopp kit was zipped up and ready, so she grabbed it, a full bottle of water and headed back to the beach. The sun was nearly unforgiving and cooked her skin the way hot oil cooked raw chicken, sizzle! She rolled her sleeves down and set her things in her luggage. She played with the lean two, but couldn't get it to stand again. Her stomach roared. "I know, I'm hungry too."

Something made a gargling sound and she looked at her stomach. "That's different." Then, there was static. "AH!" The radio, a smile blew up on her face! She shoved things around and found it. "God, how to work the thing!" She looked the knobs over, the LCD readout and then her happy expression faded. "Low battery, battery fail."

The waves rolled onto the shore. The ocean glistened and Claire panned the beachhead up to the raft. "The raft," she got up and took a step, but stopped suddenly. Goose bumps bubbled all over her skin when her eyes met the dark lump at the front of the raft. "I ... No, I can't. I just ..." She turned to her luggage. "Mark," she moved some things and got the picture of her son. His soft smile and glowing eyes comforted her. "I can't." She said and her eyes welled up. "I ... you saw what happened." Her stomach convulsed and she lay back against her luggage with Mark's picture against her bosom. "Mark, God why aren't you with me?" She wiped her eyes and sat up. "It's not a pity party." She gripped the picture tightly. "I ... it's my fault, I know. I shouldn't have taken you." She looked at his face. "I wish you would say, mom, you're fine; there's nothing to forgive." Her fingers massaged his cheek.

A bigger wave lifted the end of the raft and something toppled over, a box or container.

Her eyes widened. "Oh God, I hope it's not another ..." She looked at Mark. "You want me to go check, don't you?" She put her hand to her mouth and then looked at the raft. The corpse was a lump at the front of it, curled over onto itself. "I have to go." She and Mark's eyes met. "I love you." She set his picture in her luggage, got up and dusted the sand off her butt. "Alright, here we go." She took a step, sniffed the air and her nosed cringed! "God awful stench!" She went to her luggage. She got a scarf, sprayed some perfume on it and then wrapped it around her face. "Okay, okay, okay," she muttered, took a step, and then another step. "It's alright, just a person ... a dead person." Her steps got smaller. "A mutilated, smelly dead body." Her stomach convulsed, "right, stop talking and more walking." Her feet picked up the pace and the raft was only forty feet or so away. "Okay, okay, okay," She muttered again and her steps were more like baby steps. "C'mon Claire," her foot weighed a hundred pounds now and she didn't have the strength to lift it. "Mark!" She shouted and looked back at his picture. "I need some help."

A big wave crashed into the rear of the raft and gave it one more shove onto the beach.

"That's it, okay, okay." She got her foot up and looked at the corpse. "I can go left. I don't have to get on the front." She turned and then took another step. "Who says I have to get on the front?" Her feet got lighter, her steps got bigger and she was nearly at the raft. Then, the stench got through the scarf and the perfume. "Oh God, that's horrible!" She whimpered and her hand went up to her nose to help. "Oh, I'm sorry, but you stink!" She picked up handfuls of sand and threw it at the corpse. "God, I don't have a shovel." She turned to run away and then turned back. "I'm so close, so close." She fought the urge to give up and walked to the back of the raft. She got her feet firmly in the sand, leaned on the side of the raft and waited. "If anything, I mean anything flops out on me, I will crap, pee myself and then use words only the devil knows, so please don't do it to me." She looked up, "please don't." Her eyelids fell shut and then opened again.

Bill opened his eyes and looked at a large mass ahead of him, some lump that rose out of the water and parted the mangroves. The sun shined through and it looked like a gold colored atoll in the middle of the mangroves. "Wow," he wiped the junk from his eyes and looked around carefully. "More booby traps," his fingers wrapped around a mangrove root and held it tightly.

Claire's fingers got hold of the handle on the raft and, very slowly, she leaned up and over the edge. "Please, please, please," a seagull leapt out when it saw her! "JESUS!" She jerked back and her other hand swung wildly at the beast! Her breath fought to catch up to her fear. She looked around for the bird, "You rotten filthy bastard!" Her face darkened in fear and then anger. "You did that on purpose!" She huffed. "Damn it!" She threw the anxiety attack off and leaned back up again. Then, she looked over and the raft was empty. "Oh," there were a couple of oars, life vests and a large orange box. "Oh!" She jerked herself over the edge and hurried to the box! "FOOD!" She grabbed it and flipped the metal clasp up.

Inside were a radio, flare gun, food and water packs, first aid kit, and everything that their box had in it. "Yes! Mark, it's got everything!" She threw the first aid aside, grabbed the bags with snacks and ate up! Her hands crammed a snack bar in her mouth and then another. She stopped with a half-wrapped snack bar half way in her mouth. She pulled it out. "What about Bill?" Her stomach belched in anger! "Hell with Bill, he *left* me." Her mouth ripped the remaining half snack bar to shreds and swallowed it whole!

Bill dug his knife into a snail shell and gutted a snail from it. He looked the slimy thing over, closed his eyes and dropped it in his mouth. He vomited it right back out. "BLAH!" Spit and snail slime hung from his mouth down to the water where the dead escargot was on his way to the depths. "Dirt and salt water turd covered with slime," he spat. "Have to think positive," he laughed to himself. "I love eating mussels covered in mucous that taste like salt and dirt." His body convulsed, "got to eat something." His stomach growled under water and a rumble rippled up from his belly to his chest. "Yeah, I hear ya." He swam ahead. The little land mass pushed the mangroves apart. "What now?"

Claire ate another snack bar, looked in the sack and there was a half dozen or more left. Crumbs stuck to her lips, teeth and gums. She chewed heartily and washed it all down with warm water from the water pouch. "Ah, so good."

Bill felt his strength sliding away with every effort he made to move. That was it; he had to have something to eat or risk passing out. He was some twenty feet or so from the land mass that was mysteriously in the middle of the mangroves. "Hey," he pulled a reddish colored grape from a large tree that was on the edge of the sand next to the mangroves. "Sea grapes," he tossed a couple in his mouth. "Yes," he pulled a handful more and ate them, "not very sweet." Then, he noticed there were a couple of strings of twine that crossed his path. He grabbed another handful of grapes and ate them. Then, he sunk down in the water, reached up and plucked the first line! An arrow shot passed him, bounced off a mangrove root and disappeared into the darkness. The other twine was as thick as rope and he followed it left first, then right. The rope faded into the darkness in both directions, so there was no way to know which way an arrow was coming from. He plucked the line and ducked!

High tide pushed the end of the raft up. The waves rolled underneath the raft and bumped her. "Oh," she looked at the raft's end as it went up and down. Her heart beat jumped. "Okay, let's get going!" She quickly put everything back in the orange trunk, drug it to the side of the raft and flipped it up and over. The box landed safely in the sand. She got her legs over and fell to the sand. "Damn, why does everything hurt after fifty?" She got up, got the box's handle in hand and quickly dragged it to her spot up the beach. Then, she hurried back, got back in the raft and looked around. "Can't let this one get away," she saw a rope, followed it to the front and convulsed, "Oh dear God, that stench." She covered her nose and mouth with the scarf. Her stomach wrenched! "I know it stinks!" She kept the rope in hand and went to the back. She put one leg over and then the other. She sat on the edge and got ready to slide down. A big wave hit the raft and shoved her up and off! She landed face first in the sand. "Son of a ...!"

Bill waited and the rope hung low to him. Nothing came from pulling it. "Okay," he looked at the line, got his fingers around it and pulled!

Claire got the rope and walked way out from the raft. She looked at the man's body and turned her head. "Sorry, sorry you're dead, sorry." She half-jogged, half-walked past until the slack was gone. Then, she pulled. "C'mon!" She dug her feet in and even with the rising tide, the raft moved only a foot or so up the beach. "Gosh, you're fat!" She looked at the lean two, thought for a moment and then jogged back to it. "Okay," she got two boards and carried them back to the raft. "Okay," she smiled and had a plan. "I can do this." The back of the raft was afloat again and shifted with each wave. She got the rope, wound it around the board, and then she wound it around the other board. She quickly made a knot. Then, she made a double knot, got her feet against the boards and pulled tightly. "Ha!" She smiled and wiped the sweat from her brow. "That's enough to hold the raft to the boards, but what will hold the boards?"

The sun was headed west and shadows began to creep around the jungle and the mangroves.

Sweat built on Bill's forehead in big globules. He licked his cracked lips and didn't move. "Be my luck to stand up and then get an arrow to my head." The rope hung freely and drifted a little with a light breeze that came from the large opening in the mangroves. He got his knife out, got his hand around the rope and made a loop. The blade went into the loop and he sawed it. "Just take it easy," he cut through the rope in seconds. The ends dropped and Bill sunk low so that the water was at the bottom of his top lip. The air from his nose made little ripples on the water.

The waves were bigger yet and slammed the rear of the raft. She gulped, "the paddle things!" She trotted up to the raft, squinted at the stench and crawled in. She got the oars and life vest. Then, she threw them onto the sand just a few feet from the rotted corpse. She looked the raft over for anything else, "okay that's it." Then, she slid over the edge and dropped to the sand. "Ha, didn't get me that time." She walked off and fell over a life vest. "Son of a ..."

Bill couldn't stand it anymore. He wanted out of the water, now. "Just go," he said and slowly edged up the sand onto dry land. He kept his body low and he was halfway up the little dune. Then, his hips were out of the water, then his thighs, then his calves and, finally, his feet. He looked around and shook his head. "Must be broke."

A horrendous crack of wood tore through his nerves and he stood. Two tree trunks, over thirty feet tall, on his sides, came down!

"NO!" He leapt from the spot at the water's edge and the two trunks slammed into the mangroves! They squashed everything underneath them! Water, branches, crabs, snails and fish blasted into the air!

Bill covered his head, curled up fetal and little critters fell around him and on him! "AH!" Crabs scurried around on his back and neck; their little pointed legs made pin drops everywhere they tapped! Snails slithered and left a trail of ooze. "Get off me!" His arms flung his hands around to knock whatever critters were left off him. "Off!" He screamed, "OFF!"

Claire made several trips to get everything to her little pile of goodies. She stood tall and smiled, "I did it." The raft wasn't going anywhere. "Snack bars and water." She said and ate one.

Bill shook off the wet and got up slowly. He stood on a patch of land about thirty feet across and fifty to sixty feet long. "So, is this it, a sandbar?" Everywhere around him were mangroves. He got the pouch and took a drink of what was left. "Where to now?" He looked the letter over and then held it up to the sunlight to get a better look. "Hey," there was a faded drawing that looked like it was in-between the leather layers. "What the?" He gently turned the map at an angle and there was an image of a map beneath the lettering. "Oh man," he studied the map and angled it so that the sun highlighted the lines. "There's the beach, the stream and the mangroves." The map was clear enough now. "Just reading it in the shadows or on a table, would have never seen it … see Claire, there is a treasure map." His smile grew.

Claire made a nice place to rest and had the lean two back up. The palm fronds were across the top and she had her things neatly organized under the leafy roof. "Okay, so beds made, food, water." She looked at Mark's picture against a board and smiled. "I'm doing okay for a rich bitty." She looked at the ocean, vast and unending, in front of her. "Just need some jazz, a glass of wine and snack bars." She laughed to herself. "Got the snack bars, but no jazz radio." She chewed up another snack bar and then took a drink of water. "Radio!" She leapt up and got the yellow trunk opened. "Radio!" She shoved the safety papers, water packs and other things to the side. There, at the bottom, was another emergency radio. "AH!" She jerked the radio out and looked it over in the shadows. "Flashlight?" She dug back into the box and pulled out a flashlight, "yes!" She turned it on, looked the radio over and saw the button, "POWER." Her finger pressed it so hard that she nearly pushed the button through the case.

The radio beeped and lit up. "TRANSMITTING," tears filled her eyes and the battery indicator read, "FULL". She set it on her luggage and sat back. "Please, please be working." The ocean waves gently rolled up the beach, the birds were silent and the jungle rested. She got up and turned to the jungle. Darkness strode up the waves onto the beach and blanketed everything. "Where are you, Bill?"

Chapter 11: I'm coming back; I swear it.

"Too dark to do anything else." He took his jeans off, rolled them up for a pillow and then took a sip of water. His body forgave him the previous night on a bed of mangrove roots and rested easy on the cool sand. "Wow, look at that." The sky was littered with little bright spots, thousands of stars spread across a heavy blue darkness.

Morning, the suns orange glow crested the horizon. The heat and a lack of food and water took its toll on Bill. His pale legs glowed a miserable flat white against the sand. The sunburn on his arms, face and neck made the rest of his skin a kind of toasty dark brown color. Deep crevices formed below his cheeks, his cracked lips and his hollowed eyes.

Near the beach, the birds cawed so loudly that they rattled the palm fronds on the lean-two. Claire sat up, turned to the jungle and yelled! "Shut the hell up already!"

Creases lined her face and bits of skin peeled up. She rubbed the sleep from her eyes and looked at the horizon, "the sun isn't even up yet!" She shouted, fell back on her makeshift bed and closed her eyes.

The birds cawed quietly.

Bill turned over and both sides of his face were shadows covered with sand. A gentle breeze crept over the mangrove leaves and rattled them. His tongue dragged against the cracked bits of skin that made up his upper lip. A crab crawled up, looked him over and then darted away. The sun was high enough now that its rays touched his face, arms and legs. He yawned, sat up and stretched. "Oh man," everything around him was white or green blurs. He took in a whiff, but the air was stagnant mangrove. "It ain't that bad." Then, his stomach growled. "More grapes and water," he got up, got a couple handfuls of grapes and downed them; his throat bucked the unsweetened grapes. "Wow, talk about different in the light." He rubbed the sleep from his eyes and focused on his surroundings. The Pristine mangrove trees brown roots were anchored in the water and their crisp green leaves and solid branches looked surreal. "Trunks almost got me." The two large trunks lay quietly atop crushed mangroves.

The tiny sandbar he stood upon rose a few feet above the water and its center rose higher.

He stretched hard and then looked around. There was a mountain in the distance surrounded by coconut trees and other bushes, "volcano?" The dark leather pouch lay on the ground tucked against his jeans. "Let's see what's up next." A cool breeze caressed his bare legs. "Oh," he grabbed his jeans. "Wow, my legs look gross." He rubbed his quads and calves to get some color back or blood flowing.

Claire woke and looked at the snack bars. "Should I save some for him?" She looked at the gentle rolling waves, "helps on the way." The battery indicator on the radio read "FULL" and the readout still had "TRANSMITTING" illuminated on it. "Okay, good … good." She looked her things over and looked at the picture of Mark. "Should I go look for him?" She pursed her lips tightly out of worry. "Water, snacks and …" She looked through her luggage and pulled out a pair of walking shoes. "Forgot these were in here too." She dusted her feet off, put on some peds and the shoes. A breath of fresh air lifted her spirit. "Breakfast, then a check of my things … a spritz of Annick Goutal to liven my senses."

Bill looked at the letter at an angle to the sun's light. "So, let's figure this out." He threw a couple of grapes in his mouth and crunched them up, "so bitter." The map image under the lettering was clearer, but not so easy to

143

read through the faded leather. There was no "X" to mark the treasure spot, but there were the initials, "M.R." on a spot in the middle of the mangroves. Just beneath the initials, there were numbers: "5 by 12." He rolled his eyes, "what does that mean?" The wind caught the letter and the map's image was gone. He held it at a better angle and the map was there again. "Five by twelve?"

Claire had a fanny pack around her waist with the snacks inside it. She fastened a bottle holder to her other side, put her water in it and had two water pouches tied to her side. "Darn," she knelt and dug around in her luggage. "No, I ..." she moved every single thing around in her luggage until she scraped the bottom. "The box!" She flipped the metal clasp open and chipped her nail. "Damn it, my nail." The lid fell back and she looked all through the box. "Ah-ha!" She took out a package of tissue paper. "With the little bit I've eaten the last couple weeks, I'm not using a leaf." In minutes, she walked off and was at the edge of the jungle. The birds cawed in a raucous! "I'm not holding it!" She shouted and knelt. "It's biodegradable!"

The birds roared!

Bill looked at the mangroves around him. "Maybe it's just that." The edge of the sand bar where the trunks rested was just a few feet from him. He walked back to where he came up on the sandbar, "one, two, three," and walked five paces from there back onto the sandbar. "Five." He dragged his foot to make a line in the sand. Then, he turned a hard left and walked to the edge of the sand bar. "One, two, three, four," and so he counted until twelve which took him a few paces past his mark for five. "Okay, so I need five steps from this point." The five steps were exactly where the twelve steps met. He smiled, "it will be or it will not."

Claire finished her business, went back to her luggage and got a windbreaker. She tied the blue Lynwood windbreaker around her waist, "Helly Hansen, for the ruggedness in you." She spritzed her wrist with perfume. "Names do matter." Then, she got the picture of her son and held it up. "I'm going to go look for him." She kissed his cheek, set the picture safely in her luggage and marched into the jungle.

Bill looked thin and gaunt in his jeans and ragged shirt. His body had seen better days and was filthy. He stood over the spot where he dragged a second line and then crossed it after he walked the five paces. He shook his head, "no shovel, damn it." His hands rested at his side for a moment and then he turned them upwards. "Guys, we're this far into it." He dropped to his knees and rested for a moment. A heavy sigh pushed through his chap lips, "I hope she's alright." Then, he rested his hands on the warm sand, dug his fingers in and pulled back handfuls of sand. He made a pile of sand a couple of feet away. Over and over, he dug in, pulled back, scooped up and then dropped the handfuls in the nearby pile. He wiped tiny drops of sweat from his forehead; he needed water.

A coconut hit the ground. Claire jumped! "Damn things," she looked up at the coconut tree and the birds cawed wildly at her. "Oh, shut up already." Then, a messy wet turd hit her shoulder and splattered. She winced, turned and her eyes locked on the black, green and brown hunk of bird poop. "You dirty little … this was my last *clean* Dior from the fall collection!" She screamed.

The birds screamed back and flew around.

"My poop wasn't that messy!" She marched off and was at the stream in minutes. "Have to wash my own clothes, find my own food and then get this shi … off of me." She sighed, "that or get hit with a coconut." She chuckled and then smiled. The poop washed right out of her blouse. She let the mess drift down stream and then re-filled her bottle. "Alright, that's it then." Her hands rested on her hips as she took in the jungle; trees, brush and sandhills looked like they were ready to eat her alive! She put her foot out and walked in. "Back off, jungle." She wiped the sweat from her brow. "Humidity's eating me up."

The sun neared mid-morning in a cloudless sky and its heat beat upon every living thing.

The hole was about three feet across now and just over a couple feet deep. Sand was under every fingernail and all over Bill's hands. "Can't be that deep, the water table is close." He rested and rubbed his eyes. "Water time," he got the water, lifted it up and a few drops came out. "Okay," he let the last drops fall into his mouth and his tongue moved around quickly to get each succulent drop. His hands held the sack over his mouth even though the last drop fell out already. He looked at the pouch, "can't stop now. I'm too close."

Claire stepped over a fallen coconut tree trunk and got stuck midway over it. She teetered and gasped. "Okay!" She pushed down with her hands and lifted herself up and over the wide log. "That was awkward, yet fulfilling in a strange way." A sly smile crossed her face and she looked at the log, "was it good for you too?" A laughed blurted out, "Okay, that's it. My mind is fading. I just had a sexual one-minute stand with the dead trunk of a coconut tree." She shook her head. "I didn't even get its name." She forged ahead and looked up just once.

The sun was directly overhead and its heat bore down on the atoll, on Claire and on Bill.

Bill's face was a hard sunburned red and his skin peeled like an onion. His forearms had little tears where the burned skin was white now and peeled up in white flakes. The cracks on his skin revealed a deeper red, blood. He licked his lips; there were new cracks that bled and he tasted the salt. "Bill," he muttered. "I don't want to stop." He fell back against the sand. "I ..." He drew his forearm across his face. "Stop."

Claire walked into some thicker brush and stopped. She took a drink. "Bill!"

Bill held up his hand and it was blurry. "First signs of dehydration." He got the pouch, sat up and went to the edge of the sandbar where the sand met the mangrove swamp. "Have to," he dipped the pouch under water and bubbles came out of the opening while water went in. "Water's loaded with bacteria." He stopped, lifted the pouch, and emptied it. "Maybe near the mountain and just ... just come back." His eyes were swollen, but there were no tears. "Jesus, I ... I messed up." His legs gave out again and he fell back on the sand. "Shouldn't have come without her."

"Bill!" She yelled and the birds yelled back at her. "Stop that damn noise!" She ate half a snack bar and looked up. "Don't you dare crap on me again either!"

The sun baked his body as he lay there on the white sand. "C'mon Bill, move." He fought to sit up, but his muscles were starved for food and water. "Move!" His muscles ached, but got him up. He looked around and crawled back to the hole he dug. "Leave it ... for now, Avast matey, treasure." He half laughed, half choked. The other side of the sand bar led to the mountain; a volcano that helped make the island hundreds of years ago. "Easier to move in water," he pawed at the ground and made it to the other side. Slowly, he slid into the mangrove swamp. He looked ahead at a path through the mangroves, "seeing things already." His eyes deceived him and then they really took his imagination for a spin.

"Bill!" She stopped and looked at the jungle ahead of her. The jungle was thick and the canopy was thicker. "No, you got me once." She turned to the left and then the right. The right was dense with trees and brush as far as she could see. She looked left again. "Can't go through, go around the damn thing." She turned and marched off. "Bill!"

He stared into nothingness, that vast mix of darkness, mangroves and swamp. His eyes were set on something and he couldn't take his eyes from it. "Has to be my mind playing tricks on me." He wiped his eyes, tried to focus and then moved a few inches at a time toward the thing. "Has to be my imagination." He mumbled and stopped. His hand reached out into the air and then he let it down onto a trunk. His hand followed the trunk and it floated. He looked it over and fought the urge to feel good. "No way," it *was* a canoe. "I feel wood, rough edges, carved top." He reached inside, "hollowed out, chopped up inside." He turned and there was a rope tied from the canoe to a mangrove. He moved alongside the canoe and got his hand on the rope. "Feels very real," he pulled at the rope. "Rope … God, I hope it's not another booby trap."

"Bill!" She shouted and made her way over broken limbs, fallen coconut trees and sticker bushes. "Be out here for hours looking for him, Bill!"

He got the rope untied and pulled the raft back to the sandbar. Once there, he got on shore and looked the canoe over. There was a single paddle fashioned from a branch. There were two canteens inside, "ah!" He grabbed one and shook it with the little bit of strength he had left. Water moved around inside. He pulled the cork from the top and took a taste before he drank anymore of it. "Gross!" He threw it back in the canoe. His body gave out and he fell back on the sand. "Oh, please," he got the other canteen and it was full. He sniffed it and then took a taste, "damn." He spat it out. "Two-hundred-year-old water."

"Bill!" She was nearer the beachhead now. The waves crashed against the sand and rocks. "Okay, so I'll just follow it around and keep yelling."

He passed out on the sandbar. The hours went by in silence and the sun made its way towards the horizon.

She looked at the sun, "be dark soon." She took a drink and then turned quickly. "Okay, I hear it." She tilted her head and listened. "Waterfalls?" She walked deeper into the jungle. "The trees aren't nearly as thick here."

"THUMP!" A coconut slammed the ground.

"Damn it!" She jumped. "Stop that!"

The waterfall was just ahead of her.

"I knew I heard something like a waterfall." She looked the falls over. "How pretty."

Water cascaded down some lava rocks and into an azure pool.

She dipped her fingers into the water and then tasted them. "Oh, that's good!" She filled her bottles. "Bill!" The second bottle filled quickly. "Where the hell are you!"

Shadows came to life on the eastern side of the island and followed her west. "Bill!" She took another drink and then walked back towards the edge of the island.

Bill looked at the canteen, "Got to have some water." He looked the canoe over. "Let it go, Bill." He wiped his eyes. "Do something different or you're going to die here."

She was at the most southern tip of the island now and the sun was on its way to sleep. "Bill!" Her voice drifted into the jungle and was swallowed up. "Bill from the airplane!"

Bill climbed into the canoe and licked his horribly chapped lips. "So, they got here and left the canoe to get them out." He got the oar in hand and his hands were raw. He pushed off and the little canoe drifted into a path through the mangroves. His eyes teared up, "I'm coming back. I swear it."

Claire walked at a good pace and followed the coast line, "Bill!" Another drink and a bite of a snack bar, "Bill! Help is on the way!" She cupped her hands around her mouth. "Did you hear me, Bill! Help is on the way!"

Bill slowly drew the paddle back and his muscles cried out. The path ahead was tight for the little canoe. Some mangroves had grown back over the years and the canoe bumped the roots. "How far?"

"Gosh, how far did he go?" She sat down and rested. "Be dark soon, then what?"

The canoe, carved from a tree trunk, wound its way along the crooked path and glided smoothly through the mangroves. Shadows grew bigger and the volcano blocked the sun from the island. Orange streaks blazed across the sky above the volcano in a final shout for daylight. But, nighttime pushed onward and soon the orange streaks faded to a dim glow behind the volcano.

Bill was exhausted and his body did its best not to collapse on itself. He sighed and sniffled. The thought that he didn't get to the treasure weighed on him. He drew his arm across his nose. "Jack of all trades, master of some." He shook the sadness off. "Whatever … I just wanted to finish this on my own."

Claire stood on a cliff, looked down at the beach and then up the hill to where it went right. "It's an island." She smirked, "can't go on forever."

Bill lay back and let the canoe drift with the stream through the mangroves. The water wasn't stagnant and flowed out to sea. He looked the canteen over. "This is treasure." He touched the canteen to his forehead. "Be nice if it had her name on it … probably have 'Made in China.'" He laughed and then looked at the back of the canteen. There was something etched into the tin at the very bottom of it. "Ah," he put his fingers on the etching and ran them across it slowly. "M.R." A big smile grew and he sighed happily, "thank you, Mary." He dipped the canteen in the stream and took a swig. "Brackish, gross."

Claire made the bend and saw the very tip of the volcano. "Oh, wow." The faded orange glow behind the volcano gave it a brilliant backdrop to behold. Her legs were stout and ready. The ground ahead was a mix bag of brush, coconut trees, sand, and jagged lava rock. There was no clearly defined path; this side of the island went up and then down. "Have to make my camp here."

Darkness chased away the last of the orange glow and it was nighttime.

She set her things out and around her. Then, she got some dead palm fronds and laid them out for a bed. "Just like in South America, I remember what to do." The windbreaker made a nice blanket and she sat down, drank some water and then ate half a snack bar. "Have to start a new diet program … lost at sea on a deserted island … the mean birds' diet."

The morning sun rose, lit Claire's face up and the warmth forced her to turn away. She sat up, yawned and then looked around. "Great, I'm still here." Her hair was a jagged mess that flopped up and to one side.

The canoe rested against a large mangrove's roots. The stream drifted by slowly. Some birds cawed and that's when Bill opened his eyes. Mangrove branches hung over him, but the canopy of leaves wasn't nearly as thick. There was a coconut tree to his side and the volcano towered above the trees. "Morning," his tongue lurched around in his dry and pasty mouth. He rubbed his back. "Owe, yeah that hurts so good."

Claire looked at the remaining snack bars, four left. "Have to keep some for him." She got up and dusted herself off. A cool breeze brushed up against her and she looked around. "Cool air, warm place … storm." She quickly got her things and walked off. "Bill from the airplane!"

Bill stretched, got the oar in hand, pushed off the mangrove and continued along the winding stream. "Hope she's better off than me." He bowed, fell back into the canoe and his body gave in to malnutrition.

Claire climbed up, then lowered herself onto a ledge, walked down a path with some brush here and there. "Big mountain seems like a good place to go." She forged ahead and the morning became the afternoon. She ate the other half of a snack bar and then drank her water. "C'mon Bill. Where the hell are you?"

Bill came to and his eyes stared at the passing leaves and branches that were over him. He fought to sit up, got the oar in hand and caught his breath. The stream moved the canoe and he set the oar down. "If I die here …" He looked at the sun's rays that danced around him. "That's okay." He swallowed hard. "Man, it's an island. I mean how far across can it be?" He let the oar rest on his lap while the water carried him along.

"Bill!" She shouted and some birds cawed wildly. "Don't give me any crap. I'm looking for my …" She wondered and then she said, "friend. I am looking for my friend, BILL!" She nearly screamed that time.

Bill turned to his left and looked through the mangroves. "Claire?"

She stopped and studied the valley just thirty or so feet down from her. "Keep going," she stepped down onto a rock, then down further. "That's why they call it a jungle, because there's so much of it." She knocked a branch away and another branch took its place. "Bugs, trees, birds and heat." She wiped her face and stopped. "Bill!"

Bill heard her that time and looked through the mangroves. "Claire!" But his voice strained to say her name.

"Bill?" She looked into the brush. "Bill!"

"Claire!" He licked his lips, "Claire!"

"Bill!" She hurried towards his voice, tripped and fell to the ground. "Damn it!"

"I'm here!" He found some strength and paddled. "I'm here."

"Bill!" She shouted his name again.

"Yeah," he barely got out.

Now, she had him. "I'm coming!" She rushed through the brush and palm fronds. "COMING!"

The canoe followed the stream to the left and the mangroves thinned out. It was sand and coconut trees.

"Claire, I … right here." He said and couldn't lift the oar. "Right here," he tried to smile and the oar slid from his hands. He was in trouble, serious trouble. His body gave out and he fell back into the canoe.

The canoe drifted past the last mangrove and the stream widened.

"Bill!" She shouted and looked over the sparse sand. "Bill from the airplane?" Her eyes fought to focus and her heart beat hard in her chest. Little goosebumps bubbled up all over her arms and a cold sweat beaded up on her forehead. "Bill?" She walked on, "Bill!"

His eyes were open and the sun hovered over him as the canoe drifted along.

"Keep going to where you thought you heard him, Claire." She hurried along, a hop over that trunk, a jog here, and then she was at the stream. "Bill!" She looked over the sand, the sticker bushes, the sea grape trees, and the coconut trees frantically. "Bill, just say my name, say it once and I'll come!"

His mouth formed the word and he whispered, "Claire."

She looked all over and then stopped, "calm down." Her legs straightened, her back formed up and she drew a breath in and then let it out slowly through pursed lips. "Okay, now Bill." She closed her eyes and listened.

Bill's eye lids were so heavy and he fought them, but they came down so that there was just a slit to see through. "Help," he said clearly.

"Bill!" She yelped, opened her eyes and ran towards the place where she heard him. "Bill! I'm coming!"

The canoe drifted into an even wider stream that flowed faster to the open ocean. He found a little strength and raised hand.

She looked up and down the stream. To her left, to open ocean and to the volcano ... she focused on something that edged around the bend in the stream. "Got you!" She took off like a bull running down a street in Spain! She ran along the shoreline and there was the canoe. "Bill!" His hand hovered above the edge of the canoe! Her feet slammed into the stream and water splashed everywhere, "BILL!" She grabbed the end of the canoe with one hand and grabbed his hand with the other. "I've got you!" A smile blew up on her face and they looked at each other. "Gosh you look like hell."

"Help," he uttered.

She pulled the canoe to the shoreline and her anxiety gave her strength to pull it up. "I've got you." She set her things down, got her arms around him and looked at him. "My God, Bill."

A smile barely made the side of his cheek rise. His clothes hung on him like a flannel shirt hung on a scarecrow, no meat, just a stick.

She got him up and half carried him onto the sand. "Let's get you some water."

He drank some while she crushed up a couple of snack bars.

"You're going to be fine." She dropped the crumbs into his mouth and then helped him with water. "Have to get your strength back. Help is coming." She stopped herself and looked away.

Bill swallowed the mushy crumbs. "It wasn't your fault."

She wiped the tears from her eyes. "No, but it still hurts."

"You did all you could for him." His smile improved.

She nodded and gave him some more crushed up snack bar. "Another raft came and I got the radio working."

He nodded, "anyone left?"

She thought for a moment, "no, nobody."

By that evening, Bill was better and able to sit up. "Claire."

She had things laid out, palm fronds for a bed and had covered Bill with her windbreaker. "That's Helly Hansen."

"Okay," he tried to smile.

"Yep, from Norway. He's got the best stuff to keep you dry." She looked him over. "How do you feel?"

"Like I got the shit kicked out of me." He turned on his side and tried to stand. "I … I owe …"

"You don't owe me anything." She said quickly.

"No, I do. I'm sorry for leaving you." He managed a smile now. "I'm sorry."

"Well, we're here now … we're okay." She winked. "Did you find the X?"

He chuckled, "Yeah, but there was nothing there."

"Grave robbers maybe." She looked at the volcano.

"Well, not grave robbers, but someone got there before me … I think." He sighed. "There were some booby traps that nearly got me."

"Oh?" Her eyes widened.

"Yeah, twine strung across the mangroves." He took a drink. "I pulled one and an arrow shot at me."

"Thank God it missed you." She sighed.

"Yeah, I swore I was going back." He shook his head. "I am a jack of all trades, just a master of none."

She patted his shoulder. "Bill, you put everything you had into it. You went a long way and …"

"Came up short." He sat up.

"Not every adventure ends with what you expect." She looked up at the top of the coconut tree. "Watch out for coconuts."

He looked up. "They fall further out."

"THUMP!" A coconut hit the ground not far from them.

"Where did you find the canoe?" She looked it over.

He pursed his lips and then took a drink of water, "seems dumb, but they had all these booby traps on one side of a tiny sand bar and the canoe to get out the other side."

"Yeah, but this side has the volcano and maybe they did put some stuff, some booby traps around." She looked around them.

He looked around. "No, I believe that you had to know where to start."

The sun set and shadows came to life around them.

"I guess you'd have to have the map and the map was in the rum pit on the other side." He smiled.

"Right, so you had to start there no matter." She looked around them.

"Oh, if you hold the letter at a certain angle to the sun there is a map on the letter." He got the pouch out. "Kind of neat how they did it."

"I bet."

After they looked the map over, the moonlight was all the light there was for them.

"Better rest well tonight." She said. "The radio had 'transmitting' on it."

He looked at her with a brow raised. "That's good."

"I hope so, though I'm sorry you didn't find the treasure." She got up and lay down on her palm fronds.

"Me too." He said.

The night was quiet and they slept right through till morning when the birds cawed.

Claire turned over, "that's got to be the most annoying feature of any deserted island."

"They want us to leave." He said, got up and stretched. Despite having had some water, he was pale, gaunt.

"Don't poop." She said and covered her head with her hand.

"Excuse me," he walked behind a coconut tree.

"I did and then the dirty bastards pooped on me." She looked up with her hands over her head.

The birds cawed wildly!

"Oh, no problem there." He said and did his business.

She sat up and stretched hard. "So, head back?"

He looked the place over. "Guess," his happy spirit faded a little.

She looked at the canoe. "Can it carry two?"
"To open ocean, I guess."

"No, you said you swore you'd go back." She got up and got her things. "Let's take one more look ... before the rescue people get here."

"Before they get here?" He slowly got up.

She grinned, "Keep our hopes up, not down."

"Thank you," he went to her.

"C'mon," they hugged.

"You saved me." Bill said and barely had the strength to keep his arms up.

"Well, you saved me too." Claire said and kissed his cheek.

They drank and ate snack bars. Then, they filled their water, got in the canoe and headed back to the mangroves.

"No oar, have to use a long stick to push us." He got a crooked piece of driftwood. "Have to do."

She sat at the front of the canoe. "Seems funny that it's such a beautiful place and I want to get off this island more than anything." She pushed them along.

He sighed and closed his eyes, "reminds me of the Florida Keys."

"Never been," she pushed the canoe away from a mangrove tree.

"Pretty place with crystal clear water for snorkeling, swimming and relaxation." He looked ahead.

"If I get any more relaxed, I won't enjoy being uptight." She laughed.

Bill shook his head and laughed too. "That volcano is huge."

She turned to him. "You're not thinking of going in there for treasure?"

He laughed, "no, but the other side of the island must be hilly or mountainous."

"It is."

"With the volcano, it makes sense that this would be the way out; less appealing than the beach." He looked ahead. "Mary had something worth having with all those booby traps."

"We'll see." Claire ducked. A mangrove branch missed her head. "We don't have a shovel."

Bill laughed, "my hands worked." He sat up, "Hey, grab that ... the oar."

"Oh," she got the oar from the water and put it in the canoe. She shook her head. "No shovel?" She looked her nails over. "I already chipped a nail on that safety box."

The sun was just about at noon when they made a bend in the stream and there was the sandbar.

"That it?" She asked.

"Yeah," he pushed the end away from a mangrove and they coasted right up to the sandbar.

Chapter 12: Avast!

That afternoon, Bill and Claire got out and walked up to the hole he dug.

"That's it. There were numbers on the map, five and twelve. So, I figured they were paces, footsteps and walked them from the edges inward." He marched the steps. "See?"

"Okay," she looked the spot over. "Didn't dig very deep."

"I guess I thought that the water table was there." He wiped the sweat from his face.

"Huh?" She looked him over and then the hole.

"You know, if you dig deep enough, you'll hit water." He looked the hole over and knelt.

"I'd rather hit Dior or gold." She knelt, "Four hands are better than two."

"Okay, if you're up for it?" He walked up and knelt.
"I am."

They got their hands dug in and scooped sand away four handfuls at a time. They drug little piles of sand out and set them to the side. Bill dug in deep with his renewed strength and Claire gently pulled back sand to save her nails.

"Didn't notice them before, what are those little bumps?" She pointed at his forehead.

"Huh?" He touched his face, "oh, mosquito bites."

"They ate your lunch." She went back to digging.

"Yeah, I was neck deep in swamp water when they attacked." He scrapped his fingers across something. "Hey," he looked at her.

"What?"

"My fingers just scraped something." He pawed at the spot and then there was the top of a chest. Its dark hardwood and iron black braces showed. "Ah!"

"No shit." Claire said and dusted off the top while Bill dug around the sides.

"It's huge!" His smile hurt his sunburned cheeks. "Wow, wow."

"Yeah, be just enough room in the canoe for me and the chest." She laughed.

He looked at her and his serious expression tempered her humor. "Or me and the chest." He got his fingers around a handle and pulled, "c'mon!" The edge gave, but they had to dig more sand out. "Stop digging like a lady."

"If I get half, manicures are expensive." She said and they locked eyes.

"Seventy-thirty." He held out his hand.

"You sound like my ex-husband." She kept her hands to herself.

"I did all the work."

She held up her hands and sand fell from them. "And I'm chopped liver?"

"Sixty-forty," he put his hand to her.

"Alright," she said and they shook.

Their hands dug like mad and sand flew hither and thither. Finally, Bill got hold of the handle. "Grab it!"

Claire reached in and got her fingers on the other handle.

"Pull!"

They pulled and the large chest moved in the smallest way possible, fighting every effort that Claire and Bill put into getting it out. "PULL!"

The end gave up and the chest popped from its sandy grave. It took both of them to lift it from the hole and drag it onto the sandbar.

"So cool," Bill said and looked the antique chest over. "Now, that's a real deal treasure chest."

"Certainly, looks like it, but you know the Chinese can make …"

"Do not finish that sentence." He snapped. On the top of the trunk and carved into the wood were the initials, "M.R."

"So, Mark Read or Mary Read." She said.

He looked at the front of it and there was a large padlock. "Great, I need a hammer."

"You got that knife?" She pointed at his pocket.

"Yeah," he got it out and opened the small blade. Then, he stuck it into the keyhole, twisted it that way and this way. He jerked the lock up and down.

"If it's a hundred years old, maybe it's rusted shut." She said, got a fingernail file out and cleaned her nails.

He sat up, looked at her, "we need something finer." His eyes widened and then he snatched the file from her, "Like a file!" He worked it into the keyhole and jiggled it around. The lock popped open and he yanked it off!

"Oh my," she gasped. "So, that's it then."

"Yeah, that's it … treasure." His gaze was fixed on the iron flap over the lock eye.

She smiled, "fifty-five, forty-five."

He rolled his eyes, "sixty-forty, missy." Slowly, he got his fingers into the iron flap and tried to lift it up. "Damn things still putting up a fight."

"No lady likes to reveal her secrets." Claire looked the trunk over and kicked the lid. "Try it now."

He jumped, "thanks." His fingers got into the lip and the lid popped open! "Yes!"

Then, their excitement went dull and into half-hearted smiles.

"It's … clothes." Bill said and lifted a period piece from the chest.

"Dresses, seventeenth century. I was at a costume party …"

"Where's the treasure!" He grabbed a dress, yanked it out, and threw it to the side. Then, he grabbed a handful of other dresses. "Where?" He threw those dresses to the side, dug his hands in and to the bottom. It was all dresses. "What the hell!"

Claire got a ruby red dress with gold stitching in hand. She held it up and against her side. "Beautiful piece."

The trunk was empty and the dresses lay all over.

"There's no treasure." Bill eyes were fixed on the trunks hardwood bottom, "no treasure."

Claire picked up a satin blue dress with ash red stitching and heavy green lines that flowed down. "To a woman who had to dress as a man, this *was* treasure." She picked up a few more dresses and set them aside. "That's my forty percent and those are yours." She turned her nose up at his dresses.

Bill sat back, broken hearted. He looked at Claire and his smile and happy expression were gone.

"The trunk, the rum and the map are worth something." Claire said. "Maybe, Mark Read was a drag queen."

"Worth what, a return trip to France in coach?" He sat back and drew his hand over his sunburned face.

She handed him the water, "here, have a drink."

"I'd prefer rum." His eyes welled up.

She thought for a moment and laughed, "me too." She patted his shoulder. "Don't be so hard on yourself." She carefully folded the dresses, lay them back in the trunk and then they dragged it to the canoe.

"You found the chest." She knelt by him.

Bill looked it over, "won't fit, but it should float. You sure you want them?"

"Yes, I want them." She looked the trunk over, "I'll get you a check when we get back for your half."

"Get my forty percent appraised." He said and ate a snack bar.

"Forty now?" she said and put her hands on her hips. "So, that's it then."

"Yeah, I guess so. Forty is about it for my interest." He looked the sandbar over and then looked at the letter at an angle to the sun. "There's nothing on the map to say otherwise."

She looked at the map. "So, the map was hidden in the letter, kind of underneath it."

"Yeah, kind of." He folded the letter up. "Be worth something."

"So, maybe the real treasure is beneath the dresses?" She raised her brow.

Bill looked at her and then looked at the hole. "No, that's too easy to figure out."

"Okay, let's go then." She went to the trunk and got her hand in the handle. "C'mon, rescue boats are on the way."

"Yeah, right." He turned to her. "My curiosity won't …"

"Let you leave until you dig a little deeper?" Her smile enlivened him. He went to the hole, slid in and scooped sand away. "No, it won't."

She got the sand he scooped out and tossed it to the side. "If it's more dresses, I want them too."

"If it's more dresses, I'm going to blow a gasket." His hands, worn from digging and sunburn, bled.

Claire worked at a fevered pitch to clear what Bill threw up to her. The sun beat on them and sweat dripped all over.

"Damn," Bill's chest blew up and then down with every bit of force he used. He shook his head. "My curiosity says, that there's nothing here." He got a drink and wiped his face off.

"What did you say about the water table thing?" She moved the sand away.

"Just that we'll hit water if we keep digging." He wiped the heavy sweat from his brow.

"Or China," she laughed.

"I wondered when you were going to say that." He shook his head.

"Okay, so let's keep digging until we hit water, then we'll know." She rubbed his shoulder.

He forced a smile, knelt down and dug his hands in. More sand flew up and Claire swiped it away as quickly as she could. The sun moved west, but kept up the intense heat on them. With white sand under them and the sun above, it was hotter than hell.

"Getting cooked here," she said.

"Yeah," he sat back against the wall of the hole. Then, he looked up at her and then at his hands. His fingernails were chipped apart and sand was jammed up in his fingertips. The skin on his hands was the color and texture of the three-hundred-year-old pouch, roughhewn and dark brown. "I think …" He wiped his brow and bits of sand fell from his hand onto his face. Exhaustion beat on him.

"Don't quit now." She smiled, "I can dig."

His eyes were blood shot and welled up. "No, let's not quit." He looked his palms over.

"They'll heal." She said.

He knelt, dug his hands in and lifted out a bunch of sand. He dug his hands in and stopped. "Hey," he dragged his fingers back and scraped them against wood. "Oh, damn." His fingers raked through the sand again and dragged on wood and over iron. "Hey!"

"What?" She looked on with eager anticipation.

He swiped away the sand. "It's another chest!" He dug around the sides of it and got his hands in the handles, "not as big, but it's a chest!" He pulled and it came out easily. "Yes!"

She helped him out and there they stood looking at this much smaller chest.

"So," he said.

"So," she handed him her nail file. "Go on."

He knelt, got the file in the keyhole and gently moved it around. The lock clicked and opened. He pulled it off and set it down. "Wow, now I am shaking."

"Me too, sixty percent of that is mine." She chuckled.

He turned and looked her over, "You got the dresses." He popped the top and opened it.

"My God, Bill." Her eyes widened.

"My God is right." Bill dug his hands in and lifted out a diamond necklace that was covered with another necklace with small rubies and emeralds. There were gold bracelets with precious gems embedded in them, a pouch filled with other gems, "look at the necklaces." They were dripping with sapphires, rubies, diamonds, emeralds and pearls. He handed her a pearl necklace and got a silver coin out. "Wow, a Spanish silver coin." The bottom of the chest was filled with them. "Thank you Mary Read!"

"No shit." Claire said and put the pearls on. "You know the diamond necklace will go better with my ruby red dress."

He laughed, "We did it!" His hands shot up over his head in triumph. "YES!"

"You did it, Bill." She put her hand on his shoulder. "You did it."

By that evening, they were out of the mangroves and upstream with the small chest in the canoe and the big chest in tow. Claire had the diamond necklace round her neck.

Bill wore the blue dress with orange stitch and the pearl necklace. He had a gold bracelet on each wrist. "I feel good."

"Oh, me too." Claire said and her fingers massaged the diamonds.

"Don't know how to get this stuff back to our camp." He steered the canoe to the sand. "Let's stop."

"Drink and eat what's left." She looked back at him. "Congratulations by the way."

He smiled, "with your help."

Bill pulled the canoe up and they both pulled the big chest onto the sand. Then, they rested on palm fronds, drank and ate the last snack bars.

"Ah, this is the life." Bill said. He pulled at the side of his dress. "How they wore these things is beyond me."

"Why do you say that?" She played with the diamonds.

"Because, this thing is so heavy and the material makes my skin itch." He got up, and turned, "unbutton me."

"Now, in all my life, I never thought I'd hear that." She laughed. "You look good."

"Yeah, well itching and heat are not my thing anymore. Especially after those little devil mosquitoes ate me up." He held his arms out while Claire unbuttoned him.

"Lucky, you didn't get malaria." She pulled at the dress.

The birds cawed wildly.

"Or gonorrhea." He smiled.

"What?" She folded the dress up neatly.

"Kidding," his shirt was soaked with sweat. "Water time."

She looked at the canoe and the volcano. "If Mary put the canoe there, she had a plan to get out."

"Yeah, but to a waiting ship." He took his shirt off and hung it on a coconut tree.

"Oh," she looked up stream. "But, if we take the canoe to the ocean and oar around the island ..."

He turned to her. "What? Go around the island instead of hiking it."

"Why not?"

"Don't know if the big chest will float for that long." He looked the chest over. "It's not like it's water proof ... I think."

"So, we put the dresses in with us and drag it behind."

"I don't know." He looked at the canoe. "It's just big enough for us, the small chest and a couple things.

"Think positive," she said.

"Could stick close to the island." He looked the canoe over. "Stay one more night, then go out with the tide in the morning."

"I have no idea what that means." She got her things. "I know it's going to be dark soon."

"Yeah," he studied the trunk. "Alright, let's do that."

"What?"

"Put the dresses in with us, tie off the big trunk and then leave early in the morning." He walked towards the volcano. "I'm going to see how far it is to the ocean."

"Okay," she looked around. "Didn't you take the spear with you?"

He stopped and turned to her. "I did, but the mangroves ate it."

"They eat?"

He smiled, "be back soon." He walked off.

She looked around and then got their things together.

It was dark when Bill returned. There was plenty of moon light with a three-quarter moon. "Hey," he sat down on the palm fronds. "Comfy."

"Yes, better than sand." She had her windbreaker on. "A little cool out."

"Yep," he looked at the moon, got his shirt from the tree and put it on. "It's about a half mile."

"Okay," she felt her stomach.

"But, the water on that side is deeper and there's no beach." He pointed, "it goes into a kind of pool and then it's open ocean."

"Will it work?"

"Yeah, just have to be careful." He looked at the canoe. "We loaded up?"

"I got in with the dresses and it wasn't bad." She lay back against a coconut.

"What wasn't?"

"The weight. When … when Mark and I went to South America, we were in a raft and the guide talked about the water line."

"Oh?"

"Yes, he looked at our things and then how far the boat went down when we loaded it up." She rubbed her eyes. "My poor eyes."

"So, was the canoe's top edge close to the water line?" He got a coconut and slammed it on a rock.

"No, there was a good ten inches." She sighed. "I'm ready to go home."

"Me too," he cracked the husk. "Let's have some coconut milk."

"Oh, I forgot all about that." She sat up.

"Yep, hit the bottom like this." He slammed the coconut on the rock and the husk broke apart.

They drank the milk and Bill broke another one. "Good for energy."

They ate the coconut and drank up.

The night sky had a whitish glow from the moon's light, so there weren't as many stars to see.

Claire studied Bill and felt the words that itched her throat to come out. "Can I ask you something?"

He looked at her and grinned, "sure."

"When we were in the raft, I heard you say something about nothing underneath." She forced herself to smile, because she felt that the question was deeply personal for Bill.

He caught his breath and gulped. "Oh, yeah." He hedged.

"Well?" She persisted. "If it's too much."

"No, it's … you were open about your son." He pursed his lips. "I was …" He got up. "I was fishing with friends and we had a little too much to drink. One guy was messing with the anchor rope and got it looped around

174

my ankle."

She sat up.

"He … it was supposed to be a joke." He bit at his lip. "He held the anchor over the side and lost his grip. So, it went over and jerked me over with it."

"Oh no," she took a deep breath.

"Yeah," he gently kicked at the sand. "I saw bubbles going up as I sank and I looked at my foot, you know, to see where the rope was and saw the dark blue of nothingness."

"How terrible."

"Yeah, it was." He crossed his arms and stepped back. "It … I reached down and my hands pulled on the rope, but my eyes were fixed on the dark blue beneath me; it was a monster."

"I'm sorry to hear that happened to you."

He tightened his crossed arms. "By the time I got the rope loose, I was … I don't know, maybe fifty or sixty feet down."

She edged up and wondered what to say.

"I got the rope off and one of my friends swam down to me." He fingers were so tightly wrapped around his arm that they hurt.

"That's good."

"Yeah, but I don't remember anything else." He coughed to force the words out. "They said I drowned."

"Oh God," She got up.

"It's okay. I mean, I got over it … a little." He looked at the darkness over him. "I was so freaked out when I went in to get the raft free and then when Martin went over."

Claire gulped. "I'm … truly, I'm sorry about Martin."

"The truth is he wouldn't let it go." He said and loosened his arms. "After that, it's been easier for me to let the bad feelings go. I still don't like being in deep water, but it doesn't paralyze me anymore."

She walked over and they hugged. "Your secret is safe with me."

"And yours with me." He smiled.

They sat back down and let their minds drift to images of home as they stared into the stars.

The next morning, Bill checked that they had everything settled in the canoe. He looked at the chest and put the locks back in both of them. "Claire," he went to her.

She sat up and yawned. "Oh, is it time for our flight?"

"Ha-ha," he helped her up. "No, it's time for the end of our adventure."

Chapter 13: The End of Our Adventure

The sun's orange glow broke apart the darkness.

Bill held the canoe and Claire got in. He looked things over to be sure and then sat in the back with the oar in hand. "Alright," he set the paddle in the water.

Claire reached over and pushed them off.

The small chest and dresses were piled in the middle of the canoe and the large chest was tied to the back.

Bill oared and they were on their way. He looked at the passing coconut trees, sand dunes, and brush. "Feels foreign, some distant place you see in an exotic magazine."

"Wish it was a vacation." She said. "But, it's not."

"Here we go," Bill used the oar to steer them into the larger pool and towards the open ocean. The volcano was on their left and towered over them like some giant that guarded the doors to freedom.

They glided past and into open water. Bill's heart got a jolt of anxiety when he saw the white caps. The waves weren't terribly high, but high enough that the canoe went up and then down in sharp breaths.

"Is it going to be alright?" Claire's face, despite the dark tan, paled.

"Yeah," he didn't want to say much else and paddled heartily. "Just like we planned."

"Okay," she looked behind them and the chest was only a few feet behind the canoe. The waves rolled alongside the chest as it bobbed and rammed the water with its square frame. "The chest looks okay."

Bill paddled and tried to keep the canoe close to the coastline, but the tide fought him and dragged them further out. "Maybe," he looked right.

"Maybe what?" She fidgeted.

"Nothing, let's keep going." He dug the oar in and forced the canoe ahead.

A thundercloud hung over them and droplets came down in a soft pour.

"Better wet with rain water than ocean water." She looked at her forearms and there were little goosebumps all over. Then, she shook her head, "damn it." Her windbreaker was at her side; she quickly got it on.

"Dresses will get a good wash." He said and a wave slapped him with a spray of water. "That was fun."

The small canoe was tough and its trunk had weathered hurricanes.

Claire ran her hands over each other from nervousness and tried not to look at the waves in front of her. "I never liked being in the front of a roller coaster."

"Don't let it scare you." Bill turned the canoe to the side so that they could make their way further south. A wave caught the side of the canoe and nearly flipped it over.

"AH!" Claire grabbed the sides of the canoe and her grip made her knuckles white.

"Sorry!" He laughed, "Got to get us going south to go around." He looked at the waves ahead.

"My son, Mark, said that when we were on a roller coaster at Disney." She trembled.

"Said to go south?" He shook off the wet.

"No," She turned to him. "Don't let it scare you." A small, but meaningful smile crossed her face.

Bill turned the canoe head on towards a larger wave. "We're okay."

"I'm trying not to be scared" She still had an iron grip on the edge of the canoe.

He dug the paddle in and turned them east-south-east.

The rain got heavier and the winds pushed against them!

"Is it a big storm?" She wiped the rain from her face.

"No, we're fine." He paddled hard to keep them from going out to open sea, but the tide pulled them out anyways. His nerves jolted with every wave that forced the tiny canoe up and then let it drop with hopes to sink them.

The waves slapped the front of the canoe on the downward crash, came over and splashed inside it!

Claire used her hands to scoop out the water, but the small amount she cast overboard was refilled five times over with each wave. "What do I do?" She turned to Bill.

"We're nearly back to the beach!" The water sloshed back and forth around the dresses and the storm had tapered off.

Claire looked left. "Why don't we just go there and then drag the canoe back?"

Bill's eyes widened. "Beach and big rocks, let's try." He steered the canoe east now.

The winds buffeted the canoe and the waves shoved her round hard.

Claire looked at the outside of the canoe. "We're sinking, I think."

"Not sinking, just heavier." He looked at the dresses.

"Should I throw them out?" She wiped the wet from her soaked face.

"No," he made himself smile to comfort her. "Lash yourself to the mast, we're not done yet."

"What? What mast?" She was puzzled.

"Just hang on."

The beach was a few hundred feet away and the water beneath them was more than ten feet deep. Bill turned and looked at the big chest. It dragged behind the canoe.

"Let it go." She said and looked at the chest.

"Not yet," he oared harder and his muscles burned.

"Bill, we could lose everything." She pursed her lips and loosened her grip from the sides of the canoe. "Is it worth it?"

He stopped oaring, turned to the chest and set the oar down. "No, it's not." He got his pocketknife out, got the rope in hand and put the knife's blade against the rope. He sawed and the blade cut through the rope in seconds. The line sagged and then Bill let it go. The canoe lunged forward and the chest was swallowed whole by the waves. "That's it then." He turned back to her and put the knife away.

She smiled and nodded at him.

He grasped the oar and drove it into the water! "Been a nice conversation piece."

"You've got the other chest." She dipped her head to it.

He grinned and paddled hard.

The canoe raced along the waves, up and over each one! The beach was less than a hundred feet away. "Nearly there!" Bill shouted over the thunder that roared after each lightning strike.

Claire's eyes were fixed on the sandy beach. Her feet were ready to leap out of her shoes and get solid ground under them. "We're nearly there, yes."

The waves rolled and crashed onto the beach.

Bill turned the canoe and aimed it right at the beach! Waves tried to gobble the canoe up, but the canoe fought back!

At the beach, a big wave shoved the back up and the nose of the canoe dug in! Claire fell chest first onto the front of the canoe!

"Owe!" She pushed back.

"You alright!" Bill got them turned and the canoe slid right up on the beach.

"Yes, my boobs took the brunt." She half laughed, half coughed on the words.

"Well, God bless your boobs." Bill smiled, "We're safe."

Claire smiled and rubbed her chest. She wobbled when she stood, but the front of the canoe was on the beach.

They got the canoe and pulled it up so that it was completely out of the water. The water sloshed around inside the canoe.

"The dresses sponged up the water." She said and tried to lift one.

"Even at high tide, I think the canoe will be alright." He looked around and at the water mark on the sand. "We're far enough up … it's fine. Let's get a few things, get to our camp and take a break."

The wind blew them along and the clouds eased. Rain droplets were more a mist now and the thunder clapped on the other side of the island.

They grabbed the jewel chest and walked back. Bill plopped down on the palm fronds. "I'm wiped."

"Me too, more from stress." She took her windbreaker off. "Rains just about over."

"What happened to the lean two?" He looked at the ragged thing.

"Storm before this one smacked it down." She opened the safety box.

"Hey!" He looked at the raft. "The raft came back."

She looked and had a sly grin. "It's not the same raft. I got this box from it." She got a water pouch and a snack bar. "Here."

He drank and then ate the snack bar. "That's awesome of you."

"I'm getting good at this island living as long as we get a raft every other day." She smiled and leaned against her luggage.

"And the radio?" He looked around them. "You have it right?"

She pointed and took a drink.

"Still working, good." He looked at the clouds. "What time is it?"

"Wish I had internet." Claire said and then drank more water.

Bill laughed, "I'm sure they'd charge extra for HD here."

"Bunch of crooks, scamming millions of Americans while a few guys walk away with everything." She sneered.

"Your husband in that business." Bill shook his head.

"You guessed it. Another dirt bag among the dirt." She pressed her fingers against her head.

"Wow," he looked at the ocean. "White caps and rough seas."

"So?"

"I wonder if they're out there looking for us." He forced a grin.

"You say that and that makes me think the answer is that they gave up on us weeks ago." She looked at the open water. "So, we're really stuck here."

"No, a passing plane or ship might pick up the signal." He looked at the dark clouds.

"Might," she got a hand cloth from her bag and wiped herself off. Then, she pulled her son's picture out and set it next to her.

"You get that from your hotel?" Bill looked at the cloth.

"Hotel de Paris, Monte Carlo." She held it up. "Two wash clothes and a face towel.

"You're funny." He rubbed his hands over his face.

"For what I paid, they can deal with it." She got the other wash cloth and tossed it to him. "You think the canoe will be ..."

"The dresses are fine." He wiped his face off. "Nice towel."

"Well, now what?" She lay back against her luggage.

"Let the storm pass, get our things up here." He looked around. "Make a better shelter, find some food, we have the stream for water and survive till they come for us."

Her eyes welled up. "And if they don't?"

"You have any books in your luggage?" He smiled.

"Are you kidding, only a tablet and the battery died when it got water on it." She chuckled.

"I think our chance of rescue is better than you think." He smiled.

"You're a good man, Bill." She got comfortable and lay back.

"Thanks, though I have to tell you when I saw you at the gate ..." His smile widened.

"You thought I was a bitch." She sat up.

"You gave that poor gate agent a verbal beat down." He kicked back and rested.

"They changed my seat." She felt her face warm. "I hate change."

"Even now it upsets you." He chuckled, crossed his legs and closed his eyes.

She sighed, "No, I survived the crash."

"You did." He sat up, "Hey, why did you run to the back?"

"I read an article that in most plane crashes the front of the plane is done for." She closed her eyes.

Bill lay back down. "Wow, didn't know that." He closed his eyes, "it was true in that crash."

"Unfortunately." She pursed her lips.

They lay quiet and relaxed with cool winds that caressed them. The waves gently slapped the beach and the sound soothed them.

"Bill?"

"Yeah, what's up?" He turned on his side.

"Shouldn't we pray or something for all those people?" She turned on her side.

"We should." He stretched. "Why not chill for a little while and then we'll say a prayer."

"Okay," she kissed her son's picture.

Nighttime came and the heavy cloud cover thinned so that the stars shined through. The birds cawed quietly among themselves.

Claire sat up and looked around. She wiped the sleep from her eyes and was in a daze. The jungle was asleep and the raging storm was miles away. All that remained were gentle waves that rolled up the beach, a lite wind and a moonless sky. The dark blue was punctuated with thousands of stars that glowed a radiant white.

She panned the sky and was in awe at the sight of a sky that was unaffected by the lights of a city, "Oh, Mark you should see this." She sighed. "Just beautiful." Her body relaxed and she lay back down again. Then, her eyelids slowly shut and she was asleep again.

Bill woke. He sat up and stretched hard. "Man," he muttered and wiggled his toes. "Nice to be on dry land." The wind was a little stronger and the waves crashed a little harder against the sand. He lay back and passed out.

The next morning, Bill woke and sat up. A hardy stretch of all his limbs and he yawned. "Paradise … if we weren't stuck here." He got up, dusted himself off and looked at Claire. "Let her sleep in, today's tour doesn't start till …"

He went into the jungle, got a couple of coconuts and brought them back. "Hey," he nodded at Claire.

"Good morning." She rubbed her face and then put some water on a wash cloth.

"Breakfast." He held up the coconuts.

"Good, coconut milks loaded with good stuff." She said.

The sun was up along with the humidity.

"So, we'll get the stuff from the canoe and then figure out what's next." He took the coconuts to a large rock and slammed the first one on it.

"Alright," she looked at the raft and a sly grin came over her. "Maybe, there's some stuff in the raft to use."

"Yeah?" He looked at the raft.

"Why don't you take a look?" She smiled wider.

"I will." He tore the husk from the coconut and then cracked the hard shell.

"I know that the back is flimsy, so be careful." She pointed.

He laughed to himself. "Okay, I'll go in at the front." He brought the coconut to her. "Here."

"Thanks," she drank. "Not as good as store bought."

"Right, no sugar." He got the other husk off and cracked the hard shell. "But, it is better."

"Yep," she bathed in her devious plan to surprise him the way the corpse surprised her.

They drank up and ate some coconut.

"Hey, so why were you all about 'your people' to me?" He sat down and drank the coconut milk.

Claire nearly choked on the milk, "oh." She sat up and wiped the juice from her mouth. "I apologize about all that." She pursed her lips and didn't want to say.

"Right, but …" He said and smiled wide to nudge her along.

"So, when my son died, the local authorities, if you can call them that …
they made a lot of comments, some nasty, about the fact that I was this rich
American and they …" She caught her breath. "They wanted bribes and
things to help me get my son back home."

"What about your …"

"My husband, the jackass, was so upset with me and the whole thing that
he refused to come and help." She wiped her eyes. "I paid them and … when
I got back, some time passed and my husband had been having an affair with
…"

"A person from my people?" Bill sat back.

"Something like that." She couldn't get comfortable and turned. "I
already felt alone. Mark was …" She touched the picture. "My best friend,
my only son." She wiped her eyes with the cloth. "Every time something
happened that made matters worse, it was people that weren't in …"

"Your class?"

"Maybe," she stood and crossed her arms. "So, that started a year ago
and every time something bad happened, it just set me off."

"I hope you can find some forgiveness in …" He stood too.

"Those people?" She looked at the raft.

"Yourself," Bill said.

"We'll see." She forced a grin and that was as much as she could
manage. "It's been easier being around you."

"Good." He drank up the last of his milk and pulled at his jeans to keep them up. "I wasn't this skinny in high school."

"Start a survival show." Claire stared into nothingness. "They always lose a lot of weight."

"I'm going crazy on hamburgers when I get back." He looked at the raft. "Well, come give me a hand."

"Oh," she looked around. "My leg is bothering me."

"Suit yourself." He said, got up, and headed to the raft.

Bill headed to the raft. "God, what's that smell?"

"Oh, there were some dead fish in it!" She laughed and held her hand over her eyes.

"That's the nastiest fish I ever smelled." He was just a few feet away from the raft's nose and stopped. "What's that?" He covered his nose. "Man, that's horrible!"

"I'm sure it's nothing!" She looked at her luggage. "Wish I had my phone."

He stopped and turned to Claire. "What a horrible smell. Are you sure it's fish?"

She smiled, "What?"

He shook his head and walked up to the raft. "Oh my God, that's so *gross*!" He bent at the waist and studied the lump that was half covered by the raft. "AH!" He leapt back and fell over his own feet! "AH!"

"Did you find the fish?" She laughed.

"What the hell!" He ran back up the beach. "What the … it's a body!"

"Oh, sorry." She doubled over laughing. "Sorry!"

"You knew it was there!" His faced warmed. "Damn!" He waved his hand across his nose. "Wow, what a horrible smell, poor thing." He trotted back up to her. "That was a B.S. thing to do!"

She laughed heartily. "I know, but it was funny."

"Yeah-right, what about 'we should pray for them.'" He waved his hand at her. "Man, that stench! I'll never get it off of me."

"Alright, alright." She got a bottle of perfume. "Here, a couple of spritzes and you'll be fine."

"Right," he fanned his nose. "It's like some toxic sludge that landed on me, like grease and you never get all the grease off."

She laughed. "Now you know how I felt."

"Why?" He looked at the raft. "What happened?"

"Let's just say I got a whiff too." She spritzed him again.

"Did he die after he fell from the raft?" Bill waved his hands all around.

"No," she waved her hand across her nose. "No, he was dead long before that I think."

Bill shook his head. "Let's say those prayers."

Claire looked at the corpse, "yes, let's pray." They got up and went to the beach. They stood inches from the water, upwind from the raft and bowed their heads.

"Dear Lord, we want to pray for those people on our flight that didn't make it." He brought his hands together. "We pray for their families and the souls of those who died." He looked at Claire, "guess a moment of silence?"

"Yes," she said.

They stood there quietly and thought on the people. Then, Bill cleared his throat, "Also, Lord, I'd like to pray that we get saved, amen."

"Amen," Claire looked at Bill. "That was nice."

"So, let's get the stuff together in one place and then see if there's a way to light a fire or something." He turned from her and looked at the ocean. "Oh damn."

In the distance, a ship was headed for them.

"Look!" Claire shouted. "LOOK!"

"I see it! I hope they see us!" He ran to the safety box, ripped the lid open, grabbed the flare gun, loaded a flared and pointed it up. "We're here!" He squeezed the trigger, "POP!" The flare shot up and burst in the sky.

The ship sounded a horn!

"Oh wow, wow!" Bill's smile burst and his cheeks pushed up around his eyes!

"Thank you, God!" She raised her hands and jumped up and down!

"Holy crap, our treasure!" He tossed the gun down. "Claire!"

"What?" She kept jumped up and down.

"Let's get our treasure before they get here!" They ran off.

It was an hour or so before the cutter anchored off the coast and a runabout came for them. Several Coast Guard people helped them get their things together and loaded on the runabout.

A lieutenant waved for them to get on. "Folks, time to go."

"What about that man?" Claire asked and looked at the poor soul who was at the raft.

"We have a recovery team coming." The lieutenant said. "Let's get you on board and let the doctor check you out."

"Hey!" Bill ran to the water and went in waist deep. "The chest!" He pulled the chest up to shore.

"How about that." Claire said.

Two men helped him drag it ashore and then they loaded it onto the boat.

The lieutenant shook his head. "Not sure how to deal with this, so let's go before someone says something."

"We found it." Bill said.

"Yes, I know, but the island is technically a British Territory." He said and waved at the boat's driver. "Take us back."

Claire and Bill sat next to each other with blankets over their shoulders, her luggage, the two chests, and the dresses. They hugged tightly.

Claire smiled, "We made it."

"We did … our long journey from Paris was cut short." He sat back and chuckled.

"Right, the long short." She said.

He looked at the crew. "And the end of our adventure here."

"Maybe, you should come with me to South America." She checked her hair.

"What?" His brow rose.

"I don't want it to think it beat me." She said.

"It didn't." He said. "And your son knows it."

The runabout carried them to the cutter where they boarded with their things. Thoughts about home were no longer just something they dreamed about; they were real; they were going home with their treasures and their friendship.

The End.

About the Author:

Michael S. Lachance writes fiction and his unique and wonderous characters bring life to each scene.

Three Fools for Spies is a story about three friends who go to Europe and get caught up in a race against the Swiss police, United States secret agents, and Russian secret agents in a dangerous game of international espionage.

The Treaty of Versailles, The Power of Love is a story that evolved out of a trip to Poland and a prison camp. This story is about Erich and his love, Nikki. Prior to World War II, Nikki is arrested and imprisoned at a concentration camp. Erich will not let the man he loves die in the camp. In order to save Nikki, Erich must become what he hates most, a Nazi.

The Camera is about a priest, Father Leauvin, who is sent to the front during World War I & takes pictures of the dead & dying. He is torn between his love for Christ & his love for a woman that he met in Paris.

21 Windows is about a family who buys an old farm house in the country. They discover a painted over window and a room hidden in the house. After they knock a wall out to get into that room, bad things happen.

Currently, Michael's working on *The Adventures of Skipper Pete* (YA-four books in the series), *Butch Roberts and The African Adventure* which is about a gay man who travels to south Africa in search of fun and adventure, but winds up on the run from a rebel army.

Published works are available in eBook or paperback!

To connect with Michael, please visit

Facebook – www.facebook.com/skipper.pete

Twitter - https://twitter.com/skipperpete1

Website: www.skipperpete.com

Please join him on his website blog for updates about novels in the works, pre-orders, and Q & A. Upcoming works include: Skipper Pete Adventure Series, So Happy, and Butch Roberts and The African Adventure.

Michael's books are available as eBooks and in paperback at all major book sellers: Amazon, Barnes & Noble, iTunes Book Store, Smashwords and other sellers.

Thank you for your interest and enjoy.